"What made you think I hated you?"

Owen asked Bonnie, his mouth dropping open.

"You did," she replied, gazing at Owen expectantly.

He was clearly astounded. "Bonnie, honey," he said, his eyes holding hers, "I have a lot of ambivalent feelings about this partnership, but I certainly have never hated you. In fact, part of the problem is that I like you far too much."

Bonnie's chest swelled with a sharp intake of breath. He liked her *too much?* Suddenly she knew what the problem was—with that kiss, with everything. It was all *too much* for Owen Ketter, *too much* for a man who had been burned once before by his intense feelings for the wrong woman. He was scared. It wasn't that he wouldn't let himself like her but that he couldn't keep himself from it. Bonnie Maxwell scared the hell out of Owen Ketter—and she couldn't have been happier about it.

Dear Reader,

Summer romance . . . does anything tug at the heartstrings more? We've all experienced poignant first love at a vacation resort or those balmy summer nights on the porch swing with that special man—if not in real life, then certainly in the pages of Silhouette Romance novels, the perfect summertime reading!

This month, our heroines find their heroes around the world—in Mexico, Italy, Australia—*and* right in their own backyard. And what heroes they find, from the mysterious stranger to the charming man of their dreams!

July continues our WRITTEN IN THE STARS series. Each month in 1991, we're proud to present a book that focuses on the hero—and his astrological sign. July features the passionate, possessive and vulnerable Cancerian man in Val Whisenand's *For Eternity*.

Silhouette Romance novels *always* reflect the magic of love in heartwarming stories that will make you laugh and cry and move you time and time again. In the months to come, watch for books by your all-time favorites, including Diana Palmer, Brittany Young, Annette Broadrick and many others.

I hope you enjoy this book and all our future Silhouette Romance stories. We'd love to hear from you!

Sincerely,

Valerie Susan Hayward
Senior Editor

ARLENE JAMES

Tough Guy

Published by Silhouette Books New York
America's Publisher of Contemporary Romance

SILHOUETTE BOOKS
300 E. 42nd St., New York, N.Y. 10017

TOUGH GUY

ISBN: 0-373-08806-X

First Silhouette Books printing July 1991

Books by Arlene James

Silhouette Romance

Silhouette Special Edition

ARLENE JAMES

grew up in Oklahoma and has lived all over the South. In 1976, she married "the most romantic man in the world." The author enjoys traveling with her husband, but writing has always been her chief pastime.

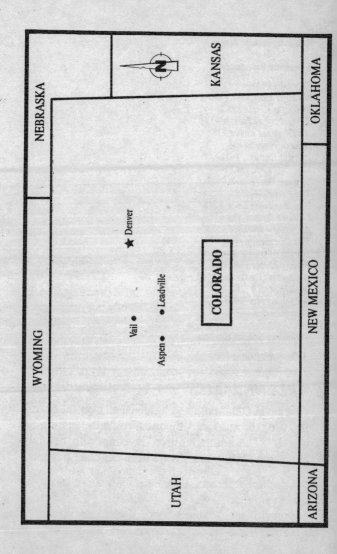

Chapter One

Owen stirred his coffee with a white plastic spoon. He'd given up cream long ago but clung tenaciously to that teaspoon of sugar per cup. It was his one remaining vice. Gone were the soothing addiction of cigarettes, the luxury of butterfat, the melt-in-the-mouth tastiness of thick beef and smoked pork, dark beer, happy hour, all-night parties, and women. He was into taking care of himself now. At forty-six, he reflected grimly, it was about time. He might be prematurely gray, but he wasn't prematurely crippled, addled, or dependent, and he had every intention of keeping it that way.

"I don't need a partner," he told the man sitting across the table from him. "I need a book full of reservations for the Christmas season."

"You need an infusion of cash," the man said, leaning back in his chair.

Harvey Pendergast cut quite a dashing figure. With manicured hands he balanced his own cup against a small

silver Christian Dior belt buckle. His paisley tie was French
silk, his dark suit Italian, his shoes hand-stitched Brazilian
leather. Owen was unimpressed. He'd worn such fashion-
ably overpriced clothing himself during his tenure as CEO
of a broad-based real estate acquisition company. It went
with the territory, territory he'd abandoned as completely
as Tish had abandoned him. The three years since that day
he'd walked out of a board meeting for the last time seemed
more like fifteen, and he'd not had a single impulse to return since then. He'd even gotten over Tish. In fact, he
liked his life. He wouldn't have a worry or a care in the
world if he wasn't three months in arrears on the lodge
mortgage. But then, with a banker for a best friend, the
outlook wasn't exactly bleak.

"Things'll pick up," he answered. "You know the entire ski season depends on Christmas vacation and spring
break."

"True," his friend agreed, "but this is only October.
How do you propose to keep it together until then?"

Owen grinned and folded his arms over the white plastic
tablecloth. "Come on, Harv. You can carry me a little while
longer."

Harvey Pendergast shook his dark, neatly groomed head.
His hair had thinned at the crown, but thanks to a friendly
and discreet stylist, retained its original color, while Ow-
en's thick, wavy hair had started graying in his twenties.
Yet, even with the silver hair, Owen managed to look
younger than his friend.

"Doesn't Leadville publish a newspaper?" he asked. "Or
do you just not read it? The banking industry's changing,
Owen. You've heard of the S & L crisis? The mergers? The
heightened federal supervision? Well, Colorado banks are
as vulnerable as the rest. The new policies are tight and
tough. I no longer operate with a free hand. No one does.

The new watchword is accountability. The easy days are over, my friend, and so is this place you laughingly call a ski lodge, unless you let me help you." .

"Aw, come on, Harv. I'm small-fry in the banking business. It's a seventy-thousand-dollar loan, for Pete's sake, not seventy million!"

"It's a seventy-thousand-dollar loan in arrears, Owen. It's been three months since you made a payment, and Archie says we're running out of track."

"Archie hates my guts, you know that!"

"Archie doesn't have enough emotion to hate anybody, Owen. He's that much like Tish. Those two aren't brother and sister for nothing. But he knows his business, and he's the boss, not that he even has much choice. The federal boys are coming out of the woodwork these days. There're two peering over every shoulder in the industry. Archie's just doing what Archie has to do, and so am I. Maybe he enjoys it a little more because it's you, but that's not really the point. You've got to do something, old buddy, either give it up or let me bring in a partner for you."

"I'm not giving up anything," Owen declared, "and I don't want a partner, especially not a woman!"

Harv just grinned. "You'll change your mind. Bonnie Maxwell is perfect for this. She's intelligent, innovative, astute, and she's got the cash, not to mention the experience. I told you she has a degree in recreation from SMU?"

Owen rubbed a hand over the back of his neck. "You told me. But I don't see how a Dallas debutante with some frivolous degree from a rich kids' school can be considered an asset."

Harvey lifted a shoulder. "Don't underestimate this woman, Owen. This isn't Tish we're talking about. She's not throwing around daddy's money for the fun of it. This is her own hard-earned cash she's investing. Bonnie Maxwell's paid her dues, and she knows what she's doing."

Owen sighed and looked around him. The wallpaper was peeling in the corner, and the rug was bare to the point of decay, and the chairs were all of the folding sort, but he'd told himself in the beginning that it was going to take time to get this place in shape. All right, so he hadn't figured it would take this long, but these old Victorian houses required a lot of upkeep, especially up here where it snowed eight months out of the year. This was a labor of love. That's what Harvey couldn't understand. It was more than just business. Still, Harv was nothing if not well-intentioned. Owen lifted his coffee cup, trying to will away his irritation. He swallowed and put the cup down again.

"So where'd she get all this experience? One of the big lodges around Denver?"

For the first time Harvey's gaze faltered. "Not exactly."

"So where was it, Harv?" Owen pressed, sensing a weakness in the other man's argument.

"What's the difference? You wouldn't recognize the name, anyway. You've been out of the mainstream so long you couldn't possibly—"

"Fine. Then let's just forget the whole thing."

"The Oaks. There. Now do you know any more than you did? You happy?"

"The Oaks. What's that supposed to mean? The Oaks what?"

"The Oaks Retirement Community! All right?"

Owen's mouth dropped open. "A retirement community? Are you telling me that the talented *Mizz* Maxwell paid her dues organizing shuffleboard games for a bunch of old geezers in visors and walking shorts? That's supposed to make her some kind of hotshot at managing a ski lodge?"

"It's an enormous place," Harvey argued, "and it's a lot more involved than you know. Think about it. How would you keep four hundred people of any age happy and entertained?"

"Holy cow, Harv! You're talking apples and oranges here!"

"Not really. The way I see it, if she can manage recreation for four hundred restless senior citizens, she can manage recreation for a so-called ski lodge that hasn't had four hundred patrons in its entire history!"

"Baloney!"

"Just give her a chance, Owen. I know she can help you make this place work."

"I don't need anybody to help me make this place work," Owen insisted, "especially not some society snob who thinks organizing sing-alongs in an old folks' home is recreation!"

Harvey rolled his eyes. "Just talk to the woman, will you?"

"Not interested."

"Just talk to her."

"Nope."

"Well, I'm afraid you'll have to," Harvey told him, sitting up straight. He delivered his coffee cup to the table and looked his old friend square in the eye. "She's driving in from Dallas today."

Owen's chair screeched across the floor, blue-green eyes going wide. "She's *what?*"

"You heard me. She ought to be here by nine o'clock tonight."

Those eyes glittered with cold blue fire. "Harvey, you sneaky, underhanded son of a—"

"Sticks and stones," Pendergast came back, raising one hand as if to shield himself. He chuckled, but there was a nervous edge to it. Nevertheless, his grin held under the heat of Owen's glare, until finally Owen looked away. Harv folded his hands and went on quietly. "I'm afraid you really have no choice in this matter, old friend, and I warn you, Bonnie Maxwell won't be as easy to get rid of as those maids you sometimes let work for you. By the way, who's doing the honors just now?"

The glare returned. "*I* am doing the honors just now," Owen muttered angrily, "and if you don't like it, feel free to stay elsewhere!"

Harvey clucked his tongue, head wagging side to side. "Not even enough cash in the till to pay the help, eh? How do you expect to hire the next maid, Owen?"

"Well, I don't expect to do it with Ms. Maxwell's cash!" Owen retorted hotly.

"Cash isn't the only thing she's got going for her," Harv stressed patiently. "This woman's smart. She's got possibilities. You'll see. Besides, you need someone to manage this place for you, someone who won't keep putting up your friends and relatives for free."

Owen smirked. "I'll remind you of that when I present you with your bill."

Harvey simply shrugged. "Put a second cup of coffee on the tab, will you? You always did make an extraordinarily good cup of java."

Glowering, Owen got up from his chair. He was a big man with muscular legs and a thick, hard chest and broad, heavy shoulders, but he moved with grace, his steps light despite the length of his stride and the bulk packed around his frame. He strode over to the shiny chrome serving table that stood in front of the kitchen door and snatched the carafe from the warming tray. He carried it back to Harvey and poured a thin, dark stream into Harvey's cup.

"Drink up, old friend," he said, "and that'll be fifty cents, plus gratuity, of course."

"Oh, you're mad as hell now," Harv shot back, carefully raising his cup, "but one day you'll thank me."

"I'll die first," Owen swore, "at a very old, ripe age, I might add." He turned and carried the carafe back to the warming tray, Harvey's companionable laughter doing nothing to dispel the gloom that was gathering about him. The last thing in the world he wanted was a partner. Correction. The last thing in the world he wanted was a *female* partner. He'd been that route and the results had been catastrophic. He had no intention of making that long journey again, no matter what Harvey Pendergast said. His mind was made up, absolutely, positively, finally, and when Owen Ketter's mind was made up, no woman in the world would ever unmake it—not again. Never.

His mind was made up. She could see it on his face, and quite a face it was, too, all sculpted gold planes and eyes like blue grass that undulated and shimmered in the sun, with straight, dark brows that jutted from a high, smooth forehead, smudges of soot against the burnished gold of his skin and in sharp contrast to the bright silver of his thick, wavy hair. Between those brows was rooted a longish nose as straight as an arrow, and below that a wide mouth with slender lips and a square chin that widened into boxy jaws. The most striking thing about this polished silver-and-gold man, however, was how at home he seemed dressed in denim and wool plaid, his sleeves rolled back to expose bulging forearms dusted liberally with dark hair. He was tall, tall enough and big enough to make her feel dainty, and that was saying something, considering that she stood five feet and ten inches in her bare feet. But very little intimidated Bonnie Maxwell. She saw that decision to refuse her in the set of his jaw and the grimness of his mouth, as well as a hint of hostility about those cool blue-green eyes, and fixed a smile on her face and forged ahead.

Harvey came to greet her across the narrow porch, leaving Owen Ketter standing in the open doorway, one strong hand holding back a flimsy metal screen door. Bonnie made a mental note about that door. It would have to go. It was completely at odds with the lacy Victorian facade of the house, but she was careful to give no such indication as she offered her hand to Owen Ketter. For a moment she thought he would refuse even the introduction, but finally his hand engulfed hers in a firm, hot handshake. He radiated heat like a stove, and a seemingly natural hostility. It was an intriguing combination for a woman who enjoyed a challenge.

"Mr. Ketter," she said, her light gray eyes engaging his easily, "I'm so pleased to meet you. Harvey's told me a lot of good things about you."

That got her a noncommital "Humph." Harvey jumped in to take up the slack.

"I've told Owen all about you, too," he said brightly, "and got just the reaction I expected."

Ketter scowled and turned away from the door, while Bonnie disciplined a quirky smile. Harvey hadn't stretched his description of Ketter one bit, but she hadn't been cowed then and she wouldn't be cowed now. It had been a long drive, fifteen hours. Her head ached slightly, and she felt an odd kind of pressure behind her face, but she suddenly felt fresh as a daisy. She went after Ketter.

"I love these old Victorian houses," she said loudly, but Ketter gave no indication that he'd heard as he strode from the small entry into what she rightly judged to be the parlor. She followed, undaunted, taking a good look around as she did so. The place needed a lot of work, but it definitely had possibilities. Offhand, she'd say Owen Ketter's instincts about this place were probably correct. His instincts about her would be another matter.

Bonnie knew what men tended to think of her at first glance. To most of them she was nothing more than a pair of long legs suitable for a short skirt. After she gave them her résumé, however, she became a pair of long legs with a frivolous degree from a snob college and suitable for a short skirt. But that was all right; a girl with three younger brothers and a strong-minded father learned early how to deal with male prejudice.

She gave herself time to take in the marble-fronted fireplace and the leaded glass in the long, narrow windows flanking it, the high ceiling fitted with wide, ornate molding, the bare, multipaned bay window looking out onto the porch, and the wood floor adorned with a thin, ragged rug.

The room itself was not bad, but the furniture looked like a bunch of garage-sale rejects. A cushioned bench with scroll legs sat against one wall, accompanied by a tall brass lamp with a fringed shade. A pair of scroll-back chairs and a small, square, dark table had been arranged facing the bench. The remaining furnishings consisted of a striped armchair, two scarred old rockers, and a horribly miscast chrome stereo system stacked around a black utility cart. She didn't have to ask who had done the decorating and hoped fervently that the rest of the house had not been similarly outfitted.

Owen Ketter sat down in the armchair, crossed his long legs, folded his arms, and stared out the bay window, leaving Bonnie standing in the middle of the floor. She didn't let it bother her. Instead, she took the scroll-back chair closest to him, dropped her small envelope bag on the floor, and prepared for battle.

"Leadville is smaller than I expected," she said by way of an opening.

"Maybe Denver's more your speed," he observed dryly.

Score one for him, she thought. She said, "Oh, I don't know. I kind of like the idea of a small town. I understand this place has quite a history."

He finally turned his head to look at her. "Quite," he said. She cocked her head in interest, but he didn't elaborate, so she folded her hands and leaned forward earnestly.

"Look, Mr. Ketter, let's just cut the small talk and get down to business, shall we?"

One dark brow rose sardonically. "All right, let's do that, Ms. Maxwell. I'll keep it short. I do not want a partner. Period."

Bonnie straightened and draped an arm over the back of the chair. Pointedly, she glanced at Harvey, who was lounging in the doorway. He shrugged, and she turned her attention back to Ketter.

"Harv said you were a tough guy to get around," she told him. "Well, I'm a tough lady. So here's my word—I can make you take me on." Anger leaped into his eyes and he stiffened, mouth opening to make a caustic reply, but she stalled him with a lifted hand and hurried on. "Archie Belton's already said he's willing to call your note if you refuse me, and I've already told him I don't do business by coercion. I'm not here to cause you trouble, Ketter. I want to help make this place a success, and I know I can if you'll only let me."

"Are you finished?" he rumbled.

"For the moment."

"I don't want a partner."

Bonnie leaned forward again. "Just give me a chance."

"I *don't* want a partner."

"You don't even know me! How can you refuse me out of hand like this?"

"It's nothing personal, lady. I just don't want a partner!"

Bonnie went straight in the chair, arm draped over the back again to look at Harv. He lifted both hands helplessly.

"I warned you," Harv said.

"But did you warn him?" she came back.

Harv chuckled. "I tried to."

She turned back to Owen. "I'll make you a deal," she began.

"Lady, I'm not interested in your deals," he said.

"My name's Bonnie. Why don't you use it? You can do me that much, can't you?"

"Bonnie," he said smartly, "I'm not interested."

"How do you know? You haven't heard my deal yet."

"It won't make any difference."

"But you'll listen, anyway, won't you? Because you're a gentleman, if for no other reason."

"Oh, brother!" he said, coming to his feet. "You're a real piece of work, Maxwell, you know that?"

"And you're not?" she came back smoothly.

He put his hands to his hips and looked down at her, but his expression was suddenly guarded, masked. She couldn't tell what he was thinking, and she didn't like that. Her father's voice sounded in her head. *First rule of business, Bonnie gal, when you can't beat 'em, join 'em.* Carefully she assumed a similar expression, giving nothing away, allowing no quarter. She slowly stood, glad she'd worn the boots with the stacked heels and the knitted wool pants with the slim legs. They made her look even taller, and she had the feeling she was going to need every inch she could get.

"Here's the deal," she said evenly. "I'll make the delinquent payments on the mortgage. In return, you let me stay and work with you through the peak season, and if I don't significantly improve business, you can tell me to get lost."

He looked at her as though she'd grown a bow on the end of her nose. "You're talking about six months!"

"That's right, from now to the middle of April."

"Six whole months!"

"Oh, come on, Ketter. A tough guy like you can stand anything for six lousy months."

"And she's willing to make the delinquent payments," Harvey reminded him.

"That'll get Archie off your back," Bonnie pointed out.

"Archie's a puke," Owen said.

"True," she agreed. "Not that it has anything to do with the price of beans. So what do you say, Ketter?"

He ran a hand down the back of his neck. "Look, Bonnie," he began, his tone suddenly reasonable, "if I wanted a partner, this would be a pretty good arrangement you're proposing here, but I just—"

"Don't want a partner," she finished for him. "Yeah, yeah, we all got that message, but if you'll pardon my saying so, it rates about the same as Archie being a puke. You may not want a partner, Ketter, but you *need* one, and my deal is as good as it's going to get. Six months, that's all I'm asking."

He looked down at the floor, lifted one shoulder then the other, sighed, looked up again. "What exactly did you have in mind? I mean, what is it you think you can do?"

She had to squelch a smile. The tough guy was weakening. "Well, for one thing, I can help you whip this place into shape before the peak season."

He smirked. "You can use a hammer, I suppose?"

"If I have to. And a paint brush, I might add. I draw the line at saws. Otherwise, I can do just about anything you can think of. One thing I can do is decorate. You know, rearrange the furniture a little, hang a few drapes, throw around a pillow or two."

"Now wait a minute," he said. "Decorating takes money, and money is just what I haven't got."

"I have my own money."

"Oh, no, you don't," he insisted. "I don't want your blasted money. If you buy in here, I'll never get rid of you!"

"Owen!" Harvey had held his peace as long as he could. "What's the point, then? You haven't got the cash to—"

"Shut up, Harv," Bonnie directed coolly. "I'm not trying to buy in," she said to Owen. "I'm trying to prove what an asset I'll be to you, but I'm going to insist that you let me do my share financially while I'm here. It's only fair. Of course, if it doesn't work out, it doesn't work out. It won't be the first loss I've suffered, and it won't be the last."

He just looked at her, hard, as though he was trying to see inside her head.

"What more can you ask for, Owen?" Harv wanted to know. "She's done everything but let you pick her pocket!"

"I don't want to pick anybody's pocket!" Owen exploded, arms flying up.

"Of course you don't," Bonnie put in quickly. "But it's beside the point. I'm nobody's idiot, you know."

"Nobody said you were."

"I'm just trying to make you understand that I know what I'm getting into," she said patiently.

"Uh-uh," he said. "You think you're making me a deal I can't refuse, but I have every intention of refusing it."

"Then why don't you?" she asked easily. He glared.

"You know damn well why!"

She inclined her head. "You need the money."

"But I don't need a partner!"

"Not even for six months?" she pressed gently. "Three months' late payments for a six-month partnership and all my expertise to boot."

"Yeah, right," he grumbled caustically. "If we happen to book a bunch of geriatric skiers, you'll come in real handy."

Bonnie had to get a grip. She looked away, forced herself to relax, and looked back, licking her lips. She chose her words carefully, enunciated them smoothly. "I'm willing to prove myself, Ketter, and I'm willing to buy myself one full season to do it in."

Something like guilt crossed his face and disappeared. "You've got to know your chances of doing that to my satisfaction are slim to none."

"I understand that, but I'm betting I can do it."

"Just so long as you know," he said.

"We're agreed, then? We have a deal?"

"I didn't say that!"

"You said as long as I knew—"

"Hold on!" Owen interrupted hotly. "Quit pushing me. Let me think!"

She'd pushed him too far, she realized, and immediately backed off. Harvey opened his mouth, but Bonnie sent him a look that positively evaporated whatever he'd been about to say. She turned her full attention back to Owen then. This was decision time, and they both knew it. She couldn't do more. He couldn't expect her to. It was just a matter of being able to reconcile himself to sharing the dream that had brought him to this grand old house. So she waited, gave him time, made no argument. Finally he looked up.

"You could lose a lot of money on this deal," he said.

"I'm willing to take the chance," she answered quietly.

"You've got a lot more to lose than she does," Harv pointed out, but Owen was concentrating fully on Bonnie now.

She held his gaze as long as he'd let her, realizing that his eyes were not so much blue-green as blue and green, that was, blue in the center, turning to a solid green at the edges. She liked those eyes, liked the shock of them coupled with those dark brows in that gold and silver face. Something felt right about those eyes, that face. He took a deep breath, breaking eye contact, then quickly reestablishing it.

"I don't want you investing more cash than I can reasonably expect to pay back when this deal falls through," he said.

Bonnie smiled. "If," she said, "if this deal falls through."

He scowled. "When. If. Whatever. I just don't want to get in any deeper than I already am money-wise, so here's the deal. Three months' payments buys you six months. Otherwise you chip in only if there's no other option and only with the understanding that I can pay you back and still call this off, *which* I'm almost sure I'll do. Now, that's it. Take it or leave it."

Bonnie was elated. It was hard not to gloat, but she reminded herself that this was just the first battle in what was likely to be a long war. She forced herself to remain impassive and stuck her hand out. "You won't regret this, Owen, I swear."

"I already regret it," he groused, surrounding her hand with his, "but I wouldn't get a better deal."

His comfortable, natural heat enveloped her, and she found herself smiling up into those blue-green eyes. There was something about this guy, something she couldn't quite put her finger on, something compelling and mysterious.

"Yes!" Harvey was celebrating, shaking his fists in the air, taking bows from an imaginary gallery as if the whole thing had been his doing and his alone. "I knew it! I knew she'd get you!"

Owen looked away, severing the tenuous connection she'd felt, and his hand dropped hers as he frowned at the gyrating banker. "Harvey, I swear, I'm gonna get a new best friend."

"Admit it, Ketter!" Harvey crowed. "I was right about this one, and you know it!"

"Everybody's right once, Harv," Owen observed dryly. "It's a law of nature."

"This is going to burn Archie's buns!" Harvey said gleefully, and for the first time Owen Ketter actually smiled.

"Let's just hope he's the only one who gets burned."

"I'm not worried," Bonnie said, and Owen gave her a look of such penetration that it startled her. Yet, even as she reached for that connection again, he pulled back. "Well, um." She felt unaccountably awkward all at once. "Wh-where do you want me? I mean, where do I stay?"

He shrugged. "I don't know. There are a couple of rooms upstairs with private baths. There are a couple downstairs, too."

"None on this floor?"

"One," he said. "Mine."

"Ah. Well, are there windows downstairs?"

"Nope."

"Upstairs it is, then."

"Right."

"I'll, uh, get my things out of the car."

He nodded. There seemed nothing else to do, so she turned around and walked out of the room, past the bench and the lamp and Harvey, who still loitered in the doorway, and across the entry. She let herself out onto the porch and closed the door.

She allowed herself a moment of exultation. She'd done it! At least, she'd gotten herself a chance to do it. She let her hand rest on a turned post at the edge of the eaves. Somehow she'd known from the beginning that this would be the place. When she'd decided to go north, she'd naturally thought of Colorado, and the idea of Colorado had naturally led her to Denver. When the investment counselor she'd consulted had suggested concentrating on smaller properties, she'd known it was the right thing to do. She wanted a hands-on situation, someplace where she could really have an impact. She could have an impact here. She'd sensed it from the moment Archie Belton had offhandedly mentioned the possibility. A ski lodge in a restored Victorian house in historic Leadville—a city born of gold, sustained by silver, and once home to millionaires, the Tabors, and "Unsinkable" Molly Brown among them—seemed perfect. It still did.

What she hadn't counted on was Owen Ketter. Oh, she'd known that Owen Ketter would be difficult to deal with. Harvey had made sure she'd known that. But she hadn't counted on the rest of it, whatever the rest of it was. She wasn't sure. She only knew just then that Owen Ketter, too, seemed—well—perfect. Maybe it was his looks, making him seem as though he was made of the lore of this place. Gold and silver, she didn't know how else to describe him. He was a tough guy, all right, but she happened to like tough guys, and they usually liked her. She hoped this one would. Anyway, she had six months to work on it. Six months in the city of gold and silver with a tough guy who could probably melt ore with body heat alone. Her headache was back, but she was too pleased to give in to it. Besides, her long trip was over, for six months, anyway—and maybe for good.

She smiled and went down the steps toward the truck.

Chapter Two

Owen lugged the two big suitcases up the front hall stairs while she carried the two smaller ones. It was just like a woman to bring everything she owned, he thought. The two he was handling felt as though they contained an entire Neiman Marcus store—each. He was almost glad they were so darned heavy. It gave him something to be irritated about, and irritation was the shield he held between himself and attractive persons of the female persuasion, one of whom Ms. Bonnie Maxwell definitely was.

Why couldn't she have been some stone-faced old maid? he wanted to know. Why'd she have to have long, black hair that hung thick and straight down her back and fell over her forehead in a wisp of spiky tendrils *and* legs that seemed to go on forever *and* the high, proud breasts *and* the tiny waist *and* the clean, pert lines of a face made of pink skin stretched over prominent bones *and*...but why go on? Thinking about it wasn't going to do anyone any good. He had to concentrate on the positive.

At least she hadn't driven up in some ridiculously expensive luxury car. Of course, a Suburban equipped with every conceivable option, including telephone, sunroof, CD player, and refrigerator, was a ridiculously expensive truck, but it made more sense than a sports car up here. Her clothing was right, too, expensive but appropriate—black wool knit slacks and a matching sweater worn without the ostentatious accessories with which Tish had driven him crazy. Bonnie Maxwell seemed to keep things simple, and he liked that. She hadn't even wanted him to sign a bunch of papers, just took him at his word, and there was no arguing that it was a good deal. It was only six months. He could stand anything for six months.

But women were dangerous. He'd learned that the hard way, and a pretty face wasn't going to make him forget it—or a shapely rear end, which was what he saw every time he looked up. He concentrated on the luggage.

"What have you got in here? Anvils?"

"Actually," she said, "it's weights."

"*What?*" He stopped right where he was, the bags balanced on the step beside him, and looked up. She laughed and kept climbing, her cute butt bobbing with every step. She reached the landing, put down the bags, turned around, and looked down at him. She was really tall for a woman, but there wasn't anything awkward or ungainly about her, and everything his eye moved over was just as firm as it should be. He put his eyes on her face and kept them there. "So you pump iron, huh?"

"Why not?"

"No reason."

She walked back down the stairs to him and took one of the bags.

"You don't have to do that," he snapped.

She smiled. "I know."

She was determined to be pleasant. How on earth was he supposed to get along with her if she insisted on being pleasant? Six months of pleasantries he couldn't stand. He let her carry the darned bag. It took both hands, but she finally hauled it up the last few steps to the top. He realized he was watching again when he should have been climbing. He hoisted the remaining bag and took the stairs two at a time.

"So what do you do?" she asked as they herded the bags along the landing.

"What do I do?"

"To stay in shape."

"I work," he said tersely, reaching for the doorknob. "This is it." He let the door swing open.

She took a good look around. He knew it wasn't much, but it was clean and serviceable. The old bed squeaked some, but the mattress wasn't lumpy. He'd painted the old iron bedstead brown and realized now that it hadn't been the best choice, but the rust didn't show. The walls were white, of course, as were the venetian blind on the window that overlooked the backyard and the blanket on the bed. The carpet was brown, but not the same brown as the bedstead, though he didn't suppose it mattered really. She and the bags took up nearly all of the available floor space, so she sat one of the bags on the rickety chair in the corner and another on the old bureau he hadn't gotten around to refinishing yet, then stuck her head in the little bathroom, which consisted of a sink, a toilet, and a tub with a shower. It was close, but it was everything she was likely to need.

"I'll have to scare up a shower curtain," he said, and she smiled.

"Great."

"The flooring in the bathroom is new," he pointed out.

"Very pretty." She nodded. "Are all the rooms like this?"

"Nope, just the singles. There are five of those, not counting mine. Then there are two rooms that sleep eight each, both in the basement, three rooms that sleep four each, all up here, and two rooms that sleep six on the main floor. It's kind of a dorm system with one bathroom for men and one for women on every level."

"That adds up," she commented. "The game room's in the basement, right?"

"Yeah, and the dining room, kitchen, and parlor are on the main floor."

"Sounds good."

"I think so," he told her. "If you want to look around, go ahead."

She shook her head. "Tomorrow. I'm really bushed. In fact, I'm so tired right now that my head is aching, but thanks, anyway."

"You want an aspirin or something?"

"No, I don't think so, just some sleep."

"You're sure that's all it is, just fatigue?"

"I think so."

"Well, if you need anything, I keep a cabinet stocked with first-aid gear in the pantry just off the kitchen."

"Okay." She smoothed her long hair with a graceful hand, and he realized there was no reason for him to stay.

"Good night," he said, backing out of the doorway. She followed him out onto the landing.

"Thanks for helping me get this stuff up here," she said quickly, "and thanks for giving me a chance."

"Just don't get your hopes up," he warned her, and she nodded again. He started away, pausing at the top of the stairs. "Breakfast is at seven," he said.

"Terrific!"

There she went again, being pleasant. He frowned and went down the stairs, hearing her door close as he neared the bottom. Okay, so she wasn't a spoiled debutante, and she demonstrated a working brain, not to mention an engaging personality, but the fact remained that she was a woman, and that was enough reason to keep his distance. Six months of keeping his distance! Well, how hard could it be? All he had to do was remind himself of Tish. She had been pleasant at first, too. He still couldn't believe he'd gotten himself married to that witch or that he'd tried to keep it together so blasted long. But it had served a purpose. Once you'd been to hell and back, you weren't nearly so likely to take the wrong road again. From now on, he was keeping himself on the straight and narrow, Ms. Bonnie Maxwell or no.

Bonnie gripped the edge of the bed and waited for the explosion of pain to subside into mere throbs of dull agony. She'd awakened minutes earlier in the pitch-black darkness, head pounding, stomach rolling, bile rising in her throat, and bolted into the bathroom to throw up the entire contents of her stomach. Now her headache was so severe, her skull felt as if it were expanding with every breath. She lay very still, willing the pain to decrease and wondering what could be wrong with her. She'd never felt like this before. Her heart seemed to be working twice as hard as normal, and there was a strange pressure behind her face.

Her stomach gradually settled, even though the pain in her head kept hammering her skull. She began to think about getting something for the headache. Carefully she sat up, feeling the pain in her head expand accordingly, and lowered her feet to the floor. She moved quickly, head held rigidly still, and slipped her hand inside the bathroom door to find the light switch. Even the indirect light spilling from

behind the door made the pain excruciating, and she had to
stop and lean her head against the doorjamb to let it subside to a bearable level before she could go on.

Eventually she was able to move around again. She dug
through her purse, looking for aspirin, then the two small
suitcases. She hadn't bothered to unpack before going to
bed because of her exhaustion, which she now realized had
more to do with this sudden illness than anything else. She
didn't find anything that would help with the headache, but
then she wasn't normally prone to headaches and hadn't
made a note to bring anything along. She thought of Ow-
en's first-aid kit in the pantry, and just the idea of going
after it was daunting, but the pain in her head reminded her
that she didn't have much choice.

She threw her old chenille bathrobe on over the football
jersey she wore as a nightgown and went out on bare feet.
By the time she covered half the length of the landing, the
pain in her head was unbearable. She stopped, grasped the
stairwell railing, and waited, head bowed, for the pain to
relent. After a while she went on, breathing carefully
through her mouth, head held at an angle. She moved down
the stairs, every step bringing a blinding surge of pain. At
the bottom she just sat down, unable to go farther, her
stomach roiling again.

"Oh. Oh-oh. My head!"

She rocked back and forth, eyes closed, and swallowed
air, trying to settle her stomach. Even the pain in her head
was secondary to the need to keep whatever was in her
stomach there. It occurred to her that she had never been
so miserable in her life, and she groaned, wishing her
mother were there. That told her something about how sick
she was. She was twenty-eight. It had been years since she'd
thought of her mother in that comforting, nursing context
that makes every little kid feel better. She groaned again

and suddenly felt a hot weight on her forehead. She opened her eyes and, in the faint light of the entryway, saw a large forearm.

"I thought so," Owen said, his deep voice seeming to boom.

"Oh, my head," she whimpered.

"Uh-huh. You don't have any fever, though." He took his hand away, and she immediately missed the warmth. "How about your stomach?" he asked.

"Awful."

"Any dizziness?"

"A little."

"Having some trouble getting your breath?"

She peered through slitted eyes at him. "How'd you know?"

"I'm a good guesser, and I had it even worse than you do, if you can believe it."

"Had what?" she wanted to know.

"Altitude sickness."

It made sense, except she'd never had it before. She said as much. He pointed out that she was in the highest city in the country, nearly twice as high as Denver.

"I hadn't thought of that," she admitted weakly.

"Smart woman like you?" he said, standing up. "I figured you'd have thought of everything."

"I'll take that as a compliment," she murmured.

"It was intended that way," he returned.

"Thanks."

"You're welcome. Now you stay right here. I'm going to get something to make you feel better."

She would have hugged him if she could have done so without spilling the contents of her stomach down his shirtfront. He left her and returned a few minutes later with a cup in his hand. He sat down on the stair beside her.

"It's warm," he said, "but it's not hot. Drink as much of it as you can. It'll settle your stomach and help with the headache. Later, if your stomach's calm, you can take something else for your head."

She took the cup from his hand and sniffed it suspiciously. It was a clear liquid that bubbled and foamed and smelled faintly of baking soda. She wanted to ask if he was sure this was all right, but she didn't have the energy, and anyway, it was worth a try. She took a deep breath, exhaled, and lifted the cup to her lips. It tasted of lemon and salt and something else she knew she ought to be able to identify but couldn't. She took as much into her mouth as she could and swallowed. It burned like fire going down, but not because it had been overheated. She gasped.

"Peppermint," he said. "Lots and lots of peppermint, minus the sugar." She was still gasping. "Keep going," he ordered, "unless you want what you've just swallowed to come right back up."

That was an appalling thought. She steeled herself for the second draught, then forced it down, followed quickly by a third.

"There, now," he said, taking the cup from her. "That'll hold you for a while."

"It had better," she gasped. "God, that's awful."

"But it works."

They sat silently for a few minutes, during which time her stomach actually calmed and the throbbing in her head diminished.

"Feel like going into the parlor now?" he asked. "I've laid a fire." She nodded and started to rise, only to feel her head expand about six inches. "Whoa!" Suddenly he was up, his arm sliding around her waist, supporting and lifting her until she could stand without swaying or doubling over.

"I-I'm sorry," she managed. "I don't mean to be a bother."

"Don't worry about it." He guided her toward the parlor, taking small, slow steps.

"You should go on t-to bed," she told him. "I'll be okay."

"Um-hm. Take the armchair." He eased her into place, folded up the shawl collar of her bathrobe, and went to stoke the fire. He came back with a light blanket that had been draped over the stereo system, apparently to protect it from dust. "I'm going to get something for that headache."

"Oh, no, don't bother. I—"

"You relax," he ordered, and walked out of the room. She marveled at the ease with which he handled the situation, then reflected that he really didn't give her much choice in the matter. She snuggled down into the chair and turned her attention to the fire, which crackled and flickered companionably.

Owen returned with two tablets and a full glass of club soda, a book under his arm. He watched her take the tablets, put the small table under her feet, and tucked the blanket into place, lowered the lights, pulled the lamp close to a rocking chair, and sat down to read. "Sleep if you can," he advised gently.

She nodded and laid her head against the chair. For a long while, no one spoke. Bonnie was warm and cozy, with her stomach settled and the pain in her head beginning to subside. She watched Owen, finding it odd that he was not dressed for bed. He'd exchanged his button-up shirt for a royal blue pullover that made the unusual color of his eyes seem particularly bright. She thought about telling him that the color was flattering, but uncertainty, combined with the coziness of the situation, prevented her. Owen looked up

now and again from his book, a bestselling espionage
thriller, but otherwise seemed absorbed. Bonnie felt her
eyes getting heavy. The next thing she knew, her stomach
was rolling and the headache was back like a brass band on
parade.

"Oh, no."

For a moment she couldn't remember where she was, but
then she saw the embers of the fire and made out the shape
of a figure crouched before them. Owen rose to his
considerable full height and came toward her, a brass ket-
tle with a blackened bottom in his hand.

"Here we go," he said, pouring steaming liquid into her
cup and handing it back to her. The aroma of peppermint
and lemon seemed to fill the room, and this time just the
smell of it had a calming effect. "Take it easy," he warned.
"It's been warming over the fire."

She lifted the cup gratefully to her lips and sipped. It was
scalding, but she welcomed the fire, knowing it would ease
the turmoil in her middle. She sent him a grateful look and
received a sharp pain in her forehead for her efforts.

"You were prepared," she said, and he nodded.

"I've had experience."

"Oh, my head." For a moment the pain was blinding.

"Keep drinking," he said. "You can have the tablets in
about ten minutes."

She swallowed liquid fire and gasped. "Wh-what time is
it?"

He didn't even check his watch. "It's nearly four in the
morning."

"Good grief! Ow." Everything seemed to hurt her head,
even strong emotion. She had her head in hand, which
made it difficult to drink from her cup, but she managed.
"This stuff is awful," she choked out, "but it works."

"That's the point." He moved over to the rocking chair and sat down.

"I've kept you up," she said. "I'm very sorry."

"No sweat," he told her. "I don't sleep much, anyway."

"Insomnia?" she asked, sipping from her cup.

"Guess so."

She laid her head back and closed her eyes. "How long has that been a problem?"

"I don't know. Four or five years."

"That's a long time to go without sleep."

"Maybe it accounts for my surly nature," he quipped.

She opened her eyes and looked at him. "You're not so surly."

"Aren't I?"

"I think you're very nice," she said honestly. The expression on his face went from relaxed to enigmatic.

"I try." He picked up his book, and she saw that he'd made excellent progress.

"You'll finish that soon," she commented.

"Um-hm."

She sipped her peppermint cocktail and left him to his book, wondering why her compliments made him so uneasy. Her head was pounding too painfully for conversation anyway, and it got nothing but worse for some time. She put aside the cup, thankful for its calming effects, and tried to relax, but the pain in her head blocked out everything else, until even her teeth and ears ached. She didn't realize she was moaning until she felt Owen's warm hand on her cheek.

"Come on, Bonnie," he said gently, and something nudged at her lips. "Let's get these down you."

She opened her mouth and felt the pills placed on the tip of her tongue. The cool edge of a glass knocked lightly against her chin, and she opened her eyes a tiny bit to guide it to her mouth. She drank the pills down with the tepid liquid.

"Gosh, it hurts."

"You've got it pretty bad, haven't you?" he said softly. "Here, let's see if this helps." He moved around behind her and began massaging her temples and scalp with his warm hands. Even with the pain, the massage felt good, and before long when the pain began to ease, it felt downright wonderful. He seemed to know when she was feeling better, for he finally stopped, his hands falling lightly to her shoulders before he moved away.

"You've taken such good care of me," she said.

"Well, I know someone who can do better," he came back.

"Really? I don't."

He sat down in the rocker, his movements heavy and slow. She knew he was tired. "I'm going to take you to see a friend of mine in a couple of hours," he said matter-of-factly. "Name's Steven Clark, Dr. Steven Clark."

"Do you really think I need to see a doctor?" she asked. "I feel so much better."

"Right now you do, but for how long? Altitude sickness can last seventy-two hours."

"Three days of this! No, thank you."

"All right, then. Let's try to get a little sleep." He wiggled around in the chair, trying to get comfortable.

"Why don't you go on to bed?" she insisted. "I really feel so much better."

"No, I don't think I better," he said thoughtfully, and crossed his arms.

"Well, then let's trade places," she prodded. "Really, I want to. I'm tired of this old chair."

He gave her a narrow look. "Just pipe down."

"Nope. I insist. Come on." She got up carefully, pleased that her head only seemed to expand three inches this time, and gave him a slightly tarnished smile. "Please."

He seemed surprised that she really meant it. "Oh. Okay. If you're sure."

She took the two steps between their chairs and bent to pick up his arm. Laughing, he rose and allowed himself to be shepherded to the easy chair. "Catch a nap," she said as he settled down. "If I need you, I'll wake you. Promise."

"All right." His expression was quizzical. "Thanks."

"What's the matter?" she said. "Don't people usually return the favor?"

"Some do."

Something about the way he said it struck her as sad. So the tough guy's been hurt, she thought. She wondered who it had been, how it had happened. She wanted him to know it wouldn't happen with her.

"Friends do," she told him. "I figure we're friends now. You didn't have to take care of me like this, and I won't forget that you have."

He just looked at her, his big, warm hands on his knees. "Whatever you say."

She smiled wanly. "I say you need some sleep."

For an instant she thought he would say something else, but then he just nodded and slid down into the chair, laying his head back. She sat and looked at him for a long time. He had the shadow of a dark beard on his jaw, chin, and upper lip, and she thought how it would scratch if she placed her cheek against his. It wasn't an unpleasant thought at all. Soon he was breathing deeply, and the muscles of his face and hands relaxed. He didn't look like a tough guy at all anymore. His lashes were long and sooty against his golden skin, his mouth fuller and softer, his silvery hair tousled. He was a big, handsome man, and he'd shown a softer, gentler side of himself in his care of her that evening. She'd meant it when she'd said that she wouldn't forget, and she told herself now that she didn't want to forget. Very much the contrary, in fact. He could be gruff and difficult, but she liked this man better all the time. If only he wasn't so guarded with her, but perhaps that would change with time. She hoped so.

She settled back in the chair and turned off the lamp by which he'd been reading, and the two of them sat there in the firelight, he sleeping, she watching and rocking and thinking. The pain in her head had left it feeling empty and light, but otherwise she felt very much her old self. Around daylight, the ache began to make itself felt once more, and she knew she would be wise to go and dress now while she was still able to do so. Quietly, she made her way upstairs, where she brushed her teeth and washed her face and combed her long, sleek hair before stepping into a pair of rust-colored pants and a roomy, matching sweater with a cowl neck. She rejected the boots for a pair of dark green canvas slippers, took her purse, and started back downstairs.

The ache in her head was more pronounced now, and her stomach was feeling rubbery, but what troubled her most was the speeding beat of her heart and the accompanying weakness. She had to go carefully down the stairway, both hands on the banister, and by the time she got to the bottom, her head was truly pounding again, so much so that she felt it would be wise to sit down for a bit. She had only just got down, though, when Owen walked in from the back of the stairs. He'd shaved and pulled on a red-striped sweater. A long gray scarf hung around his neck.

"Here," he said, holding out a tan overcoat. "I thought you might forget yours."

"I thought you were sleeping," she told him.

"I was," he returned, "but I woke up in time to give Steve a call. He's on early rounds at St. Vincent Hospital, but said we could meet him there. From the looks of you, I'd say we'd better get a move on." She nodded wearily and began pulling herself up by the banister, feeling her stomach start to roil again. He draped the big coat around her shoulders and slid his arm about her. "I think we'd better take your truck," he said. "Mine's out back, and if we try to make it that far, I have a feeling I'll be carrying you."

"The key," she mumbled, opening her purse. They were out the door and moving across the porch before she found it. It had snowed sometime the night before, just enough to spottily cover the ground, but she was surprised that she hadn't noticed it falling past the window. "We need lots of that, don't we?" she said softly.

"What?"

"Snow," she murmured, "lots and lots of snow."

"Don't worry," he said, helping her down the stairs. "You'll be sick of it before you leave here."

"But I don't want to leave," she told him. "I just want my head to stop hurting."

"I know the feeling." He took the key from her and opened the passenger door. "Up you go."

She felt herself being lifted, and her arm went automatically about his neck, but then he was putting her down on the seat and buckling her belt. He withdrew and closed the door before hurrying around to let himself in on the driver's side.

"I do feel better," she said, seeking to reassure him. He started up the engine and looked at her.

"That's not saying much."

"I guess not."

He put the car in gear and backed out of the little parking area. She put her head back and closed her eyes. Four minutes later he was pulling up at the emergency entrance of the little hospital.

"Feel like walking in?" he asked.

"I think so."

He came around and helped her down, then guided her up the ramp and through the door. Minutes later she was sitting in a treatment room alone when Dr. Steven Clark came in. "Ms. Maxwell, is it?" he said, reaching for his stethoscope.

"Bonnie."

"Owen tells me this is a nasty case of altitude sickness. Let's see if he's right. Deep breath, Bonnie, please." The examination didn't take long. Dr. Clark—or Steve, as he told her to call him—chatted all the while he shined lights, fingered her glands, and counted her pulse rate. He was a nice man, tall, but not as tall as Owen, and slender, with brown hair and eyes. His smile was bright, and his bedside manner smooth and breezy and upbeat.

"Looks like Owen's right again," he told her with a forced sigh. "We're going to give you an injection and a couple of prescriptions. Next time you go flatlanding, let me know beforehand and I'll give you something you can take to prevent this. But remember, you have to take it *before* you start back. Deal?"

"Deal."

"Great. I hate to see a beautiful woman suffer." He winked and grinned.

"Thanks."

"Don't mention it." He headed for the door. "While the nurse is taking care of you, I'll be outside giving Owen a hard time."

"Don't give him too hard a time," she said. "He got me through the night."

He chuckled. "I didn't think the tough guy had it in him." He went out, and moments later the nurse came in.

She stuck a needle in the top of Bonnie's leg and injected the medication, then helped her into a wheelchair and pushed her down the hall to where Owen waited in a tiny lobby. Steve was with him, but he turned and came to meet her, taking over the wheelchair and sending the nurse away with thanks.

"Partners," he said, obviously having gotten the whole story already. He stopped the wheelchair in front of Owen, who was standing with his hands in his pockets. Steve clucked his tongue. "And here I was thinking Owen had actually found himself a woman!"

Owen scowled and addressed Bonnie, who was already beginning to feel the effects of the injection. "The guy thinks he's a comedian and all his best material concerns my private life."

"Hey," Steve protested, "I'm an optimist! I say where there's life there's hope, but I should have known you wouldn't have sense enough to date something this gorgeous." He leaned down and spoke sotto voce into her ear. "The truth is, this guy's been inoculated, but I haven't. I'm terribly susceptible to a pretty face, and yours is one of the prettiest I've seen in a long time."

"Don't get excited," Owen grumbled. "He flirts with voices on the radio."

"Just the female voices," Steve defended poutily, and Bonnie giggled. "I believe the medication is having its desired effect," he told Owen. "Better get her home while she's still conscious." He pushed the chair to the door, and there Owen helped her up and to the truck. She was feeling definitely light-headed, but she remembered to thank the doctor. "My pleasure," he called out the door, then he turned the chair around and disappeared.

"Nice guy," she said as Owen all but lifted her into the truck again.

"Umm," was his only reply. She meant to ask him about Steven Clark, but by the time he had the Suburban on the road again, her tongue had grown thick. There was no ache in her head, and her stomach felt only slightly rubbery. Moreover, the pressure behind her face seemed to have gone. She was asleep even before they turned toward the house.

Chapter Three

Bonnie stretched and rolled over in bed, coming awake. She felt wonderful, like a lazy cat with no reason to get up except to lap cream. The only leftover of her illness was a slight headache. The stiffness of her muscles she attributed to a longer than usual sleep, which caused her to wonder what time it was. She reached for the small, leather-encased travel alarm sitting on the floor beside the bed, lifted it, and read the dial. Six o'clock. She looked at the delicate light filtering through the window. Apparently she had slept nearly twenty-four hours.

She barely remembered getting into bed and didn't remember at all getting out of the truck and coming upstairs. She supposed she had something else for which to thank Owen Ketter. The thought made her want to get up and go downstairs. Carefully she sat up, throwing back the covers. Had she removed her own clothing and put on the football jersey? She decided that she had. No worry there. She put her feet to the floor and slowly stood up. The ache in her head did not seem to increase, but her stomach rumbled emptily. She dressed in mustard yellow slacks and a matching blouse accessorized with a paisley scarf and went downstairs, wondering if Owen would be up.

He was sitting in the dining room, at the end of one long table, the collapsible sort that could still be found in some public schools. A rectangle of thin, white plastic served as a tablecloth, and before him were a plate, a paper napkin, a fork, and a knife. In one hand he held a folded newspaper, in the other a stemmed glass containing a dark red liquid, which she supposed could be cranberry juice.

"What are you drinking?"

At the sound of her voice, he looked up, simultaneously stowing the paper and lifting the glass. "Wine," he said. "I'd ask you to join me, but you really shouldn't be drinking now."

Bonnie walked to the table and stared down at the place setting he had made for himself. Salt, pepper, bread sticks, Parmesan cheese mixed with bread crumbs, a small bowl of some green herb. "This isn't for breakfast," she noted aloud, and he chuckled.

"Breakfast? Try dinner. Pasta shells stuffed with chicken and cheese and served with marinara sauce, to be exact. You'll be hungry, of course."

"Starved," she admitted, "and confused. How long did I sleep? Ten, eleven hours?"

He laughed outright. "More like thirty-five or thirty-six."

She put both hands to her head. "No wonder I'm so hungry!"

"Well, your timing's good," he said, getting up. "It's almost ready. I'll bring another plate."

She followed him into the kitchen, still marveling at the length of her "nap." She looked around her and immedi-

ately went from one marvel to another. She was no cook,
but this room had obviously been fitted by one and an ex-
pert cook at that. Shiny stainless steel reflected light from
a dozen different surfaces. Pots and pans hung from racks
suspended from the ceiling. An array of ovens filled half of
one wall. Open shelves were lined in military order with
every conceivable accessory and tool. Small baskets of
vegetables and jars of herbs were strewn about, and there
must have been three dozen cookbooks arranged in a glass-
fronted cabinet beside a worktable with a marble top.

"Wow!"

"Like it?" he asked, taking plates down from another
section of the cabinet.

"I've been in restaurant kitchens that didn't measure up
to this!"

"Thanks." Leaving the plate on the counter, he grabbed
an oven mitt and went to check the oven. As he opened the
door, a delicious aroma filled the room.

"This is great!" she said, meaning room and aroma, as
well as the promise of excellent food. "Who did it?"

He sent her a slightly offended look. "I did."

This was a pleasant surprise. "You're the cook?"

"None other."

She couldn't have been more pleased. "Harv said the
food was excellent, but he didn't say who cooked it." She
sniffed appreciatively. "If it lives up to its billing, I'd say
we have an unexpected asset here. Where is he, by the way?
Or doesn't Harv eat dinner?"

Owen extracted the dish from the oven and sat it on a hot
pad on the counter so he could peel away its tin foil covering. "Harv flew back to Denver yesterday," he told her.
"Said to say, 'So long and good luck.'"

"I thought he'd stay longer," she commented, trying to
peek over his shoulder.

"Harv's not very good at relaxing," he told her. "He wanted to get back to the office."

"That stuff smells wonderful," she said, dismissing Harvey Pendergast.

Owen took the bubbling dish from the oven and showed it to her with obvious pride. The pasta shells were as big as her palm, stuffed with what looked like a tasty chicken salad, and swimming in bright red sauce. Her stomach gurgled appreciatively.

"We'd better get some of this in you!" he exclaimed. "Grab the plate and flatware and follow me."

She did as told, practically treading on his heels as he carried the white ceramic baking dish to the table. He made her sit and wait while he spooned the shells and sauce onto her plate and topped them with Parmesan, bread crumbs, and a pinch of the chopped herb. He poured her a glass of water, sat down, and watched as she cut into the first shell, blew onto the steaming morsel on the tip of her fork, and popped it into her mouth. The flavor was heavenly, a creamy blend of tender chicken, ricotta, and vegetables, accentuated by an excellent tomato sauce rich with garlic.

"I have a new favorite," she announced, diving in for her second bite. "My compliments to the chef." He was smiling so broadly that his blue-green eyes crinkled at the outer edges, and two shallow creases marked his cheeks. "You have a nice smile," she told him sincerely, and it instantly evaporated. She was stunned, a little hurt even. Silently, she concentrated on her meal, while he did the same. After a bit, he paused to lift his glass.

"I'm glad you like the pasta," he said quietly. She put on a smile and nodded. He went on. "And I'm sorry I'm so touchy."

"Why are you?" she asked, her fork momentarily stilled.

He shrugged. "I don't know... Well, I do know. I just don't know how to explain it."

Bonnie settled her gaze on his eyes. "Who was she?"

He blanched, then dropped his gaze to his plate, but at least he gave her an answer. "Archie Belton's sister, my ex-wife."

"Oops."

"And now you know why he was so willing to call my note."

"What I don't know is why you gave him the opportunity," she said. "I assume it was an ugly divorce."

"Ugly marriages beget ugly divorces," he muttered.

"And Archie naturally took her side?" It was as much statement as question.

"He helped her help herself to just about everything I owned," he said. "Stocks, bonds, mortgaged properties. I thought all that stuff was supposed to be held jointly by husband and wife, and Archie was only too happy to use his position to help me set it up that way—I thought. What he'd done was make it possible for her to clean me out just before she filed for divorce. I was broke, divorced, and homeless all in the same day."

"Sounds like she caught you by surprise," she observed.

"You could say that," was the bitter reply.

"But if it was a bad marriage you must have known the possibility of divorce existed."

He shook his head glumly. "I was a genuine dope. I bought it all. Marriage was forever. So what if the going got rough? You stuck it out, worked it out. Right?"

"That's the idea," she agreed.

"Wrong. Maybe that was the idea once, but not anymore."

He went back to his dinner, that implacable statement hanging between them. Bonnie didn't know quite what to say. He'd obviously been crushed.

"You must have loved her very much," she finally said, but he only looked at her.

"I don't know," he told her. "I thought so, but now I just don't know. I mean, what is love, anyway? It sure isn't what I thought it was."

"Maybe you tried it with the wrong person," she suggested gently.

"Maybe I did," he said, taking up his fork once more, "but I can tell you one thing—I won't be trying it again."

She wanted to argue with him, tell him that he was cheating himself and some lucky woman out of a lifetime of happiness. But who was she to tell him how to live his life? Besides, the look on his face told her that it would be a waste of breath, and she really couldn't afford to antagonize him. She ate her pasta and tried to understand the depth of feeling that produced such depth of pain as Owen's. It told her something important about this man who had become, temporarily at least, her partner. How many women were waiting for a man capable of such emotion, herself included? She decided she would have to deal carefully with Owen Ketter, for her own sake as well as his.

After what seemed an appropriate length of time, she brought up the subject of business. She made some astutely worded suggestions about changes she felt the house needed, and the discussion carried over into a detailed tour and cataloging of the premises. Their empty dinner plates abandoned, they moved animatedly from room to room, discussing and sometimes arguing about what needed to be done.

In a nutshell, Owen disagreed less with what she proposed than with the idea of her putting up money to implement the changes. Bonnie was careful not to push, using instead the techniques of encouragement that she had learned while earning her degree. Owen Ketter could be led only so far, however. He was one "client" who required logical, sometimes irrefutable argument before he could be swayed, and on some points he couldn't be swayed at all. Such was the case when they came to the subject of the game room.

"The room must be finished," she told him, gesturing at the unpainted walls and the bare concrete of the floor, "and the sooner the better. Let me call in a contractor and get it done."

"No way." The set of his mouth told her it would be pointless to argue further, but she felt quite strongly about the need to get the place in the best possible shape.

"Owen, please be reasonable," she said lightly. "It doesn't require a great deal of material, and the right man could make fairly short work of it. It needn't cost a fortune."

"It needn't cost anything right now," he rebutted. "I'll get around to it."

"With what?" she asked. "Can you afford the materials?"

He shook his head. "Not right now."

"Then let me do that much, please. I mean, we're partners, after all. I'll provide the materials. You provide the labor. That's fair, isn't it?"

"It's fair, but you know how I feel about it. I just can't afford to get in too deep with you. When the time comes to split, I want to be able to make a clean break."

"And what if the time to split doesn't come, Owen?" she countered gently. "What if we turn out to be a great team? You are going to give me the chance to prove myself, aren't you?"

He seemed clearly uncomfortable, but in the end he agreed that he had every intention of allowing her to prove herself. "But I don't intend to do it by going into hock with you."

She felt defeated, but she made herself be a good sport about it. "I don't want that, either. I just want this place to be a success. I want to do the very best that I can for this partnership."

To her surprise, that seemed to make an impression on him, and she stored away another bit of information about Owen Ketter. He was not only a man capable of intense emotion, but also a man able to respect it in others. He licked his lips and recanted.

"All right, if you feel that strongly about it. But we're going to keep this within reasonable limits. You can buy the materials, but only the materials I say. Agreed?"

"Agreed!" She wasn't about to push for more, and this, too, seemed to appease him. They talked over what was needed—paint for the walls and cement floor, some sort of floor covering for the television area, acoustic ceiling tiles, trim to finish out the door frames. "We could paint the floors in the rooms down here, too, make it part of the decorating scheme, and then buy a few throw rugs and mats, you know, something between your feet and the cold floor."

"One problem," he said. "We don't have a decorating scheme."

Not yet, she thought. She said, "Oh, right. Well, what do you want to do about the floors in the rooms, then?"

He seemed to think it over. "We might as well paint them," he said. "The rugs can come later."

"Sounds reasonable." She smiled, but he frowned. It was suddenly as if she'd overstepped, come too close, agreed too readily. She immediately withdrew. "We can leave the rooms until later, if you like, or paint them all the same color as the rec room. Whatever makes you most comfortable."

He was still frowning. "Maybe we should paint them all the same color as the rec room," he grumbled. "I-I'll pay you back as soon as I can, maybe when I find a real partner."

A *real* partner? Bonnie bit her lip. She was surprised by how much that hurt and reminded herself that it was silly to feel that way. She'd known from the beginning that he didn't want her, and she'd certainly given him no reason as yet to change his mind, getting sick like that, keeping him up all night. She swallowed down the hurt pride and strengthened her determination.

"If that's the way you want it," she told him evenly. Still the frown did not leave his face. She looked away and heard him sigh.

"Bonnie, I know you have high hopes," he began, "but I'm not sure you're looking at this thing realistically. I just don't want a partner. This is my place, and while I appreciate your enthusiasm and your input, I still can't say that I want to share."

"I understand," she said, "but if you must take a partner, why not me?"

It was his turn to look away, and he seemed to be ducking the question. "I wonder if you even realize what you're in for? I mean, you say you want a hands-on situation, but the kind of help I need may be more 'hands-on' than you're willing to get."

"For instance?" she asked.

"For instance, somebody's got to keep the place clean and change the beds and do the laundry."

She lifted her chin. "I can do that, a lot of it, anyway."

"We're talking sweeping and mopping and vacuuming here."

"But no cooking," she teased. "I mean, I cannot cook. As silly as it sounds, I just never learned. I've lived this long on cereal and the kindness of friends."

At last he smiled. "No wonder you're so skinny."

Her reaction was natural, unconsidered. "I'm not too skinny!"

"I didn't say you were *too* skinny," he came back quickly. "Truth be known, I envy you. Not only do I love to cook, I love to eat, and on a guy my size, every extra pound looks like fat."

"It all looks like rock to me," she told him honestly, and instantly the frown returned.

"Yeah, well, let's just say I have the cooking end covered and leave it at that, okay?"

"Okay." Once more she felt deflated.

"I'd better clean up the dinner dishes," he muttered, but she was quick to object.

"Oh, no," she told him, stretching out her hand in emphasis. "Cleaning up is my job. Besides, I owe you for taking care of me last night."

"Night before last," he reminded her.

"Right! I still can't believe I slept so long."

"You were pretty sick."

She took a step forward and lifted a hand to his shoulder. "I don't know what I'd have done without your help," she told him.

He looked uncomfortable but did not move away. "I didn't see much choice about it."

She lifted her hand to his face. He seemed to steel himself, as if to keep from flinching, but for some reason she could not make herself take her hand away. "You had a choice," she said softly. "You could have gone to bed and turned off the light, left me to deal with it myself. But you didn't. You stayed up all night pushing that repulsive drink on me, and then you took me to your own doctor and let yourself be ribbed about it and brought me home and helped me to bed and let me sleep. You may be a tough guy,'' she went on, ''but you're a tough guy with a big, soft heart, and I'm very grateful for that.''

It was then that she noticed his gaze had fallen upon her mouth, and for the first time she thought that he might want to kiss her. She felt strangely calm about that possibility and yet excited, too. It was as if her heart smiled, and somehow she knew that if he did kiss her, it would be very right, very sweet. She waited to see what it would be, and after a moment, he switched his gaze to her shoulder and then to the floor. A sad disappointment filled her, but she lifted her chin, telling herself there would be another time, and lightly kissed him on the cheek.

He stepped back, face reddening, and she instantly regretted the impulse. She started to apologize, but he cut her off. ''Y-you better get on those dishes,'' he rumbled, turning toward the stairs. He rubbed a hand over his face and started up, then he halted. ''Come on,'' he said, ''I'll show you around my kitchen.'' Not *our* kitchen or even *the* kitchen but *my* kitchen. Still, it was better than nothing.

Bonnie smiled and quickly followed, covering the sadness she felt. It was going to be very hard to reach this man, to make a partner of him, and it was such a shame because she felt that they could be more than partners, more even than friends. But hard was not impossible, and she was a long way from giving up. *So hold on, buster,* she told his broad, rigid back, *because here I come.* Still, she knew she'd have to watch her step with Owen Ketter. He bore wounds that had not yet healed, and the last thing she wanted to do was reopen one of them. She wanted to help, not to hurt, now more than ever.

Owen let himself in the back door, kicked the snow off his feet on the mat in the mudroom, hung up his jacket and knit cap, and walked into the back hallway. A left turn took him into the kitchen, whereas a right would have taken him into his own bedroom. He stuck his head in the door and looked around before going directly in. It was a bother, checking out his own house before he walked around in it, but it was more of a bother running into Bonnie Maxwell unexpectedly. That woman got under his skin, and the fact that she tried not to didn't help at all, neither did spending her money.

He hated taking her money, hated even that she'd opened the charge account for him at the building supply outlet, but what else could he do, having promised her a chance to turn this place around? He comforted himself with the idea that he'd pay back every lousy cent, but that came with the uncomfortable knowledge that he'd only be able to do that if she actually accomplished her goal, and if she accomplished her goal, how could he then in good faith turn her away? It was a mess, and he was angry with himself for getting into it. He should have stood his ground.

And lost the place? he asked himself. Archie would be only too happy to make that happen. He never should have gone through Harv to finance this place, but at the time he'd felt Archie owed him. Now it was the other way around. And he had nobody to blame but himself, the realization of which did nothing whatsoever to cheer him.

Morosely, he made himself a sandwich with the leftover turkey breast he'd roasted the night before. That and an apple constituted lunch. He was still munching the apple when he went out into the dining room. Bonnie was nowhere to be seen, so he walked through the entry to the parlor. What he saw there made his mouth fall open, snagging Bonnie's attention. She was standing on a chair in her bare feet, hanging a green curtain, her arms stretched out in front of her, her dark hair pulled back by a folded bandana. She looked over her shoulder.

"Oh, hi! What do you think?"

What did he think? What did he *think?* "I think you're out of your everloving mind!" he told her loudly.

She let the curtains droop and turned around. "What?"

"What?" He knew he was overreacting, but he couldn't believe she had done this without asking. He twisted about, taking note of the damage. Every stick of furniture had been moved. The rug had been replaced! There were pillows and cushions everywhere. The armchair wore a new slipcover to match the curtains she was busy hanging. The fireplace now had a freestanding screen, and some sort of low cabinet stood in the corner. And where the hell was his stereo table? "How dare you just . . . turn my house upside down!"

"Owen," she said reasonably, getting down off the chair, "you said I could decorate as long as—"

"You've spent a fortune in here!" he exploded, anticipating her argument. "The deal was that you wouldn't spend more money than I could reasonably pay back."

"They're borrowed, Owen. Everything's borrowed."

"Oh, sure. From whom?"

"From me!" she told him bitingly. "I haven't bought a thing I can't take with me if I leave."

"When you leave!" he shot back automatically, only to see a wounded expression tighten her face. She quickly mastered it, but he'd seen enough to evoke a sharp stab of guilt. He looked away.

"All right," she said, "if that's the way you choose to think, go ahead, but it really doesn't have anything to do with what I've done to this room, and we both know it."

His hackles went right back up. "What you've done to this room is an invasion of *my* home!" he exclaimed, shaking his half-eaten apple at her.

"Rot!" she came back. "If you'd cool down enough to really see this place, you'd know it looks 110 percent better! And it isn't just *your* home. It's also *our* place of business—for now, anyway."

Which it was, of course. He glared at her, but then made a point of taking a good look around. He'd missed a few things at first. She'd brought in a couple of potted plants in small brass tubs, and the lamp had a new shade fringed in the same silvery green as the drapes. An old-fashioned oil lamp stood just to the center of the mantel, and there were a couple of small round tables with marble tops that complemented the fireplace front. The rug underfoot was a dark pine green embellished with a pattern of intertwined vines and a wide fringe in the lighter green of the drapes. Some framed prints had been grouped on the wall. It all looked rather elegant and without seeming feminine. And it was true that every item, from the rug up, could be packed and hauled away in short order. He didn't know quite what to say, so he bit into the apple and chewed furiously.

"Don't you like it?" she asked in a small voice that made him cringe.

"It's all right," he muttered, but the unfairness of that immediately began to eat at him. "Actually," he amended, "it's pretty good." She beamed, so delighted with even such faint praise that he felt irritated with her all over again.

"It would look even better if we could paint," she told him enthusiastically. "For the busy walls with the windows and doors, I was thinking maybe we could pick up the melon in the chair covers. Then the rest could go this wonderful dark hunter green, and the celery we could use for the trim to kind of tie it all together. Wouldn't that look great? People would just love to sit in this nice, peaceful room after an exciting day on the slopes, have a little fire, you know, and maybe some soft music. The stereo, by the way, is in that credenza there.''

He walked over and lifted the lid. His stereo tuner and the CD player rose on hinged shelves to within easy reach. The speakers, he noticed, were hidden by large hinged grids on either end of what was essentially a chest, and his modest collection of CDs filled a portion of the vertical shelf. A couple had been added. He took them out of their sleeves and read the titles. Nothing he could argue with here.

"These yours?" he asked.

"Yes, and I have a few others in the truck, if you're interested."

"They'll come in handy," he said. "Reception isn't very good in these mountains."

"So I noticed."

He put the CDs back and closed the lid, saying, "I have some things to bring in."

"Could we talk first?" she asked carefully. He sent her a discouraging glance and could tell that she was nervous, but that didn't seem to make any difference. "Please," she went on. "It's important."

He nodded and turned to fully face her. "What's it about?"

"I don't know what to call the place," she said, shrugging. "I mean, for starters, is it actually a lodge or a bed and breakfast inn?"

"Sort of half one and half the other," he replied.

"Well, that's what I thought, too," she said excitedly, "so I thought we could call it a bed and breakfast lodge."

"Makes sense," he agreed.

She seemed greatly relieved. "Thank goodness," she said, clapping a hand to her chest, "because that's what I told the bank."

Bank? "What bank?" he asked, suddenly suspicious.

"Well, *the* bank. I mean, the one downtown."

"What has that bank got to do with us?" he demanded.

She gave him a blank look. "Owen, we talked about this," she said calmly. "I told you I was going out to open some accounts."

It dawned. "You opened a *bank* account?" He couldn't believe it. "In whose name?"

"Name? Names! In our names, *both* of our names!"

He rolled his eyes. "That's absurd! *We* don't have any money."

"Of course, we do! A little, you know, for operating expenses."

"You call this operating?" he shouted, expecting her to beat a hasty retreat. To his surprise—and pleasure—that pretty little chin came out. Cool gray eyes suddenly snapped at him.

"You are being impossible!" she said, deliberately stressing every second syllable. "You're just mad because I haven't given you any reason to throw me out yet. I've done exactly what you've asked me to. Every investment has been a prudent, necessary step in getting this place together, and as far as I'm concerned, what I cannot take with me—*if* I go—will just be chalked up to poor judgment. You won't owe me a cent, not one copper penny! Now cool it! Or so help me I'm going to show you what mad really is!"

He felt his brows shoot upward. So she wasn't yet really mad? He couldn't help wondering just what mad would look like on her. As it was, she looked like a kitten trying to bare its claws, an incredibly attractive kitten, but a kitten, nonetheless, a fact that he was only now realizing.

"So how old are you?"

At the sudden question, she could only gape at him.

"What?" He said nothing, as surprised as she by the turn of the conversation. She blinked, apparently digesting the question at last. "I-I'm twenty-eight. What has that got to do with anything?"

Twenty-eight. He remembered twenty-eight. He'd thought he could do anything, be anything, and be it and do it better than anybody else. Was it really eighteen years since he'd been twenty-eight? He felt old and disillusioned at forty-six, and for a moment, looking at that trim, lovely, invulnerable young woman, he knew the sharpest, coldest, most bitter envy he'd ever experienced.

"Owen," she said, the sharpness in her voice replaced by wariness, "what's this all about?"

"Nothing," he mumbled, suddenly wanting desperately to be away from her. "The, um, room is fine." She just looked at him, and he felt something stir in himself that he'd thought long dead, something that scared the hell out of him. "Do what you want about the...bank. I have work to do," he finished quickly, and then he turned and got out of there, striding through the entry and into the dining room.

And not a moment too soon, he told himself angrily, pushing on into the kitchen. *You're losing it, old man, and you know better. Oh, man, do you know better.* He strode on through the kitchen, the hallway, and the mudroom, not pausing to grab his jacket or cap before bursting out into the clear, chilly sunshine. He felt his feet sink into the snow, felt the sharp cut of the air. It was getting colder. It would snow again tonight, snow on the mountain. He felt better already.

Chapter Four

Bonnie renegotiated her position in the armchair, tucking one bare foot under the opposite thigh, and flipped the page of the magazine she had been trying to read for the past hour or more. From beneath her she heard and felt the muted whump-whump of the hammer as Owen nailed boards in place to form a grid for the ceiling panels. Her thoughts went immediately to the room below, zeroing in on the tall man standing on the low scaffold, muscled arms raised over his head, the fabric of his white T-shirt stretched like a second skin over his hard torso. With a snort of self-disgust, she tossed the magazine aside and lurched to her feet, beginning to pace.

She hated the silence between them, his grudging, mute acceptance of her and her money, and she hated that she wanted so desperately to make peace. She reminded herself that she'd already tried a truce that evening. When she'd realized that he was going to stay down there working right through the dinner hour, she'd impulsively run out and picked up a couple of delicious burgers from a little place on the edge of town. He'd accepted the food with the same inelegant gruffness as he'd accepted the redecorating of the parlor and the opening of a business account. No one she'd ever known had made being right less agreeable for her, and here she was about to ask for the same treatment again. And yet she couldn't just let it stand as it was between them. Something just wouldn't let her leave it alone.

She stepped into her shoes, expensive little leather flats that pinched her toes and rubbed her heels, their hard soles too slick to allow her much freedom of movement. She didn't know why she continued to wear them, except that they were the perfect color of fuchsia to accent the diagonally striped pink and purple knit of pants and top she wore. Gingerly, she made her way out into the entry and down the stairs to the floor below. Near the bottom she took a moment to compose her face.

Owen was standing exactly as she had pictured him. He looked over his shoulder as she came across the floor toward him, one hand supporting a short length of lumber, the other groping for the hammer hung in a loop of the leather tool belt slung about his hips. Without a word she skipped quickly to his side, lifted the hammer free, and held it up to him. He gave her a blank look beneath his upraised arm, took the hammer from her hand, and pounded home the nail he had already set in the board.

"What are you doing down here?" he asked, taking another nail from the pocket of his belt.

"Just thought I'd help out," she replied, linking her hands behind her back.

"I can manage," he said, and the nail he was about to set slipped from his fingers. "Blast!" He went into his pocket for another, but Bonnie was already bending, reaching for the nail.

"Here you go." She straightened and lifted her arm. Owen took his hand from the pocket and slowly reached for it.

"Thanks."

"Sure. What else do you need?"

He set the nail and looked down at her, arms lowered to his side. His expression was frank and a little puzzled. He motioned to the worktable he'd fashioned by laying a sheet of plywood over the pool table. "You could hand me that square."

She wasn't exactly certain what a "square" was, but a quick glance over the table told her there was only one instrument lying about that could measure a perfect ninety-degree angle. It was flat, made of metal marked in increments, and shaped like an L. She took it to him. He lifted it into place, checking the position of the board before pounding home the second nail. Bonnie was ridiculously pleased with herself.

For some time she played fetch-it, going for and handing up various materials as he set several more short cross-members. Her shoes were hurting her, but not sufficiently to make her step out of them or go up and change. She and Owen were actually working together, and she didn't want to ruin it by skipping off just when he needed her.

Owen nailed the final crossmember of that section of the grid in place and walked down the narrow beam of the low scaffolding he'd built about two and a half feet off the floor. He moved quickly, with a lightness of step and athletic grace seldom seen in a man of his size, to the opposite end, where he dismounted in one long stride. A long board cut into two sections lay on the floor, and he bent to pick up one end of the first piece.

"Think you can help me lift these into place?" he asked, and Bonnie hurried to take a position at the opposite end, nodding vigorously. "Okay, now here's the plan," he said, balancing his end of the eight-foot-long section against his knee. "It isn't particularly heavy, but it's unwieldy, so it takes a bit of coordination. We step up on the scaffold, me first, then you, lift the board over our heads, and slide it between the guides I've already nailed in place. The ends should butt up to those two beams. Then I'll secure this end and work my way toward you as fast as I can. All you've got to do is stand there and hold your end in place until I get to it. Got it?"

"Got it," she confirmed, and he nodded.

"Let's go, then. Me first." He stepped up on the scaffold, his end of the long board rising slowly. Bonnie followed, surprised that such a thick board would bow so easily. "Together now," he instructed, and Bonnie lifted the board with him, her head going back as it rose so that she could watch its careful progress. "Between the guides now." The guides were small blocks of wood. With great effort, Bonnie helped him slide the board between the four pairs of guides. It was a perfect fit. "Now hold on."

Holding on proved easier said than done. It would have been easier if she'd been able to extend her arms all the way, but her elbows remained at the level of her ears, bent just enough to keep her from using the strength of her forearms to aid her. Still, she managed to hang on as Owen quickly nailed the board to the beam at his end and then the first two pairs of guides. Her feet were hurting and her arms were trembling by the time he got to the third, then, just as he struck the first blow on the nail he'd set in the fourth, her whole body shuddered. One foot slid out from under her, aided by the slick sole of her shoe, and suddenly the beam on which she stood rocked from side to side. She heard a clunk, felt the beam sliding away beneath her. Suddenly Owen's arms were around her, and she bumped into his chest as they went down together, somehow managing to stay upright.

They wobbled, legs entwining, and Bonnie had lost a shoe, but the floor was beneath their feet, if only she could find it. Her arms were flung about his neck, and she tightened them, instinctively using his warm, solid body for support. And then they were still, his arms locked tight about her waist, hers about his neck, legs tangled so that they stood hard against one another. Bonnie was so delighted not to find herself on the floor that she did not at first grasp the significance of the situation, until she lifted her gaze to his, intending an effusive thank-you, breathless with relief. Breathlessness was all she managed, for the instant she met those blue-green eyes up close, she knew exactly what was about to happen, so that even as his head tilted to the side, hers was moving forward.

Neither of them closed so much as an eye at that first gentle meeting of their lips. It was as if each waited for the other to chicken out, but for Bonnie any thought of pulling away was banished the moment his mouth settled over hers that second tentative time. An indescribable sweetness flowed over her, sweeping her straight into an ecstatic oblivion where sensation thrived and conscious thought could not go. Instinctively she loosened her hold, turning her hands into the thick wavy hair at the back of his head, moving her mouth and body against his, feeling him doing the same. His big hands splayed over her back, pressing her against him. His mouth melded smoothly with hers, as their noses met, parted, and met again. Some tool in his belt pressed into her groin, and even that was pleasurable to the point of eroticism. Then, suddenly those small, accommodating movements exploded into broad, feverish motions that threatened to overwhelm, and just as suddenly she felt herself roughly thrust away. She stumbled backward, eyes wide, too stunned to think.

Owen glared at her accusingly. "It won't work!" he shouted. "Do you see now that it won't work?"

She didn't know what to say. "Owen, I . . ."

"Stay away from me," he demanded raggedly. "Stay away from me!"

"I—I will," she promised, backing away. "I'm sorry, I . . ." But it was no use. He had turned away from her, was bending and snatching up her shoe. He thrust it at her, gaze turned away, chest heaving. She picked it carefully out of his hand and hurried with a slightly lopsided gait to the stairs, where she paused long enough to slip it onto her foot.

She wanted to say something, do something, to make him understand how important it all was to her, how important *he* was to her, but Owen Ketter didn't want to be important to anyone. He didn't want to know how she felt, and he certainly didn't want to feel anything for her. Not that he was obliged to. This was supposed to be business, after all, business and nothing else. She went up the stairs without another word, determined not to think or question or worry. She didn't dare, not now, for she wanted too much from this man, more perhaps than she even realized.

She did think, of course, and she questioned and she worried. It was impossible not to do those things, but in the end she was able to put it aside. After all, what had taken place between them had not been her doing alone. He had kissed her as fully and as willingly as she had kissed him. And he had liked it. That much she knew. Perhaps he had liked it too much.

At any rate, it hadn't been a smart thing for her to do with so much at stake. Failure here wouldn't be the end of the world. She could go elsewhere, try again. One way or another she would make something of herself, do something with her life. She had been raised for that. It made no difference whatsoever that her family had a bit of money, more than a bit, actually. What mattered was *doing* something on one's own, whether it was feeding the orphans in India or helping to create the finest little bed and breakfast lodge in America. It was just that she wanted to do it *here*. Something about this place felt like home to her. And Owen needed her. He couldn't admit it yet, but Owen needed her. He needed her smarts and her style and her encouragement. Her money was such a small part of what he needed from her and what she could give. She wasn't going to let one kiss mess it up.

Wisely, she did as she'd promised and kept her distance. It wasn't easy. Owen was the only other person in the house, not that they weren't going to have guests eventually. There were some reservations in the book, and she felt certain that they would receive more, but she wanted that book full, and she intended to do everything in her power to make it so. That gave her a dual purpose for getting out of the house, to give Owen the space he felt he needed and to find ways to promote the lodge. She was certain that Leadville had more to offer than history, though to be sure its history was rich, indeed.

The famous names associated with the community were legion. It seemed that everyone from Susan B. Anthony to Oscar Wilde had sojourned for a time in what was once a wildly successful mining base of the strike-it-rich variety. Stories could be told of such luminaries as Sarah Bernhardt, Doc Holliday, and Buffalo Bill, not to mention a number of millionaires and politicians.

Little was left of the grandest mansions that once faced Leadville's streets, but many of the smaller, less opulent homes had survived in one form or another. They were

known as "Painted Ladies," these colorful, graceful, prim
houses with their intricate "gingerbread" trim, porches,
and steep gables. They were a joy to view, and Bonnie could
just imagine what a picture they would present at Christmas. But Leadville, though small, had much more to offer
than fanciful architecture.

In short order Bonnie compiled a long list of restaurants
and bars. She also found adequate shopping for essentials,
every necessary service, well-stocked sporting goods stores,
and a host of interesting art galleries and antique shops, not
to mention more than a dozen churches, video rental out-
lets, a small airport, a golf course, a car rental agency, an
excellent little bakery, and as many as six interesting mu-
seums, though not all were open all year. More interesting
still were those entries made under the heading of Recreation and Entertainment.

At various times of the year, it was possible to go bicy-
cling, bowling, fishing, rafting, swimming, horseback riding, and, of course, skiing—cross-country or downhill—as
well as snowboarding. One could ice-skate, snowmobile,
pan for gold, toss horseshoes, hit a golf ball, and go for a
surrey ride or a sleigh ride or even a carriage ride, the lat-
ter two being accompanied by a candlelight dinner. Live
theater was offered at the fabled Tabor Opera House. The
Chamber of Commerce presented a slick multimedia show
chronicling the community's history, and in the proper
season a visitor could tour the area by train, horse, Jeep,
bicycle, or snowcat. In addition, the community boasted
indoor facilities for swimming, racquetball, basketball,
therapeutic massage, and weight training. It was also possible to enjoy a hot tub or a whirlpool spa. The year's calendar was crowded with event after event, everything from
the International Pack Burro Race to the Leadville Music

Festival, the Boom Days Celebration, and the Victorian Christmas Homes Tour.

Bonnie felt as if she'd struck her own vein of gold. There was enough here to keep the reservation books full the year round, if she and Owen so chose. All that was required was to get the word out about what Leadville had to offer. It was necessary to advertise. Given enough time, word-of-mouth would probably fill the place to the rafters, but her time was limited and the clock was, as they say, ticking. Advertisement, however, would be expensive, especially as she envisioned it, so there could be no doubt that Owen would object. Nevertheless, she determined to propose the idea—at the right moment, whenever that might be.

It was days before Owen even spoke to her again, beyond those words necessary to conduct daily life, anyway. She did not offer to help him again, but used her time researching the community and cleaning the house. The evenings were the worst. The days seemed to fill themselves, but the evenings invariably stretched into long, lonely ordeals. Her mere presence was reason enough for Owen to absent himself. Therefore, her presence in the parlor necessarily deprived Owen of the stereo, just as her presence in the rec room cost him the use of the television. She didn't want to deprive Owen of anything, so her only option was to sit in her room and read. Thankfully, Leadville boasted an adequate bookstore.

Along about the fourth day after the catastrophic kiss, as she'd come to think of it, Steven Clark, the doctor, stopped in to say hello. Bonnie was overjoyed, not because she'd even thought about the doctor during the past week, but because for the first time since their shared kiss, she and Owen were compelled to sit in the same room and make conversation. Owen was his usual taciturn self, but he played the part of host with quiet congeniality. He even poured them each a beer and served them with soft, hot, homemade pretzels as big as Bonnie's hand. Steven teased Owen about his "passion for cooking," and Bonnie heard herself defending him.

"We'd both starve if he didn't cook," she admitted, "and I'm betting his expertise will bring us a lot of repeat business."

Steven smiled into his mug at that. Owen seemed to hide behind his. Bonnie felt her face flush and wondered if she'd said something unintentionally risqué.

"I wonder if Owen's expertise will keep you from having dinner out with me one evening," Steven said by way of an invitation.

Bonnie knew suddenly that she didn't want to go out with the charming Dr. Clark, but she felt uncomfortable about turning him down. Would he think that her relationship with Owen was more than a simple business arrangement if she declined to have dinner with him? Would Owen think that she was intending such a relationship with him if she did not accept? She glanced at her reluctant partner, and to her irritation found him looking relaxed and amused, more so than at any previous point during the visit. She didn't know why that irritated her so, but it made her mind up.

"Dinner out would be lovely, Steven," she said evenly. "Would sometime next week be all right? There's still so much to do before the season opens on Saturday."

He was obviously surprised. "Great! I'll call you, and we'll set something up."

Bonnie nodded and slipped a glance in Owen's direction. His expression was guarded, uncertain. His eyes were on his beer. She felt a keen sense of disappointment, and yet she couldn't have said what she'd expected. Steven was talking still, and she applied her attention to him.

"We could even drive over to Vail. Wouldn't take more than an hour," he said. She shook her head, glad to have something concrete to add to the discussion.

"I'd really rather try one of the local places," she told him. "It's important that I be able to make intelligent recommendations to the guests."

"All right," he agreed readily. "We'll go someplace you haven't already been."

She laughed. That wouldn't be difficult. Other than the one carry-out hamburger, she hadn't tried any of the local fare. She told him so, and they chatted about the possibilities. At one point Steven turned to Owen and asked his opinion. Owen merely shrugged.

"What possible difference could it make to me?"

For some reason, that stung Bonnie, but she tried not to show it. Steven laughed and chalked it up to Owen's conceit about his abilities as a cook. Owen said nothing. A little while later Steven took his leave. Bonnie accompanied him to the door. As she returned to the parlor, Owen left it, bearing a tray stacked with dirty mugs and serving plate. He did not return.

They had two guests, a couple of scraggly looking young men, and eleven inches of snow on opening day. Their guests were not interested in breakfast, dinner, or anything else except skiing and drinking. The skiing was not particularly good, despite a fifty-six inch powder base, because of the rapidly falling snow, but that didn't seem to make any difference to their boarders. What seemed to matter was being first on the slopes. They returned after a day of what must have been near-blind skiing, showered, changed, played a raucous game of pool, complained about the lack of video games, and went out to find a bar. They returned some time before daylight and left shortly thereafter.

The next day turned out to be beautiful. The snow spar-
kled under sunshine so crystalline that it hurt the eyes. The
trees, evergreen and majestic, their sweeping boughs bur-
dened with snow, stood as still as paintings. The fields lay
quiet and serene beneath white blankets stitched with fenc-
ing, their meandering streams hidden from the crisp, clean
air. The pale blue sky seemed to be held up by a founda-
tion of white, billowy clouds that curled against the brown
and green peaks of the surrounding mountains. Between
the fields and the mountains lay the little city, with its
church spires and narrow streets.

Bonnie stared from her bedroom window, enthralled by
the view, when she heard the series of metallic clunks coming from the yard below. Her forehead against the glass
pane, she turned her gaze downward and spied Owen
loading skis, boots, pack, and what looked like an overlarge skateboard into the back of his truck. At once she felt
a leap of excitement. The lodge was empty. The day was
perfect. He was headed for the slopes. She wondered if she
might be allowed to go with him and saw, to her delight,
that he was returning to the house instead of getting straight
into the truck.

Quickly, she tied back her hair and went out of the room.
She found him in the kitchen, his big hands wrapped
around a cup of coffee, which he sipped while leaning
against the counter. He wore a green bib over a white turtleneck and a coat appliquéd with blue and white patches.
A green stocking cap and white insulated gloves lay on the
countertop.

"Well, I see great minds think alike," she quipped. "I
was thinking of hitting the slopes myself. It's a beautiful
day, isn't it?"

"Um-hm." He sipped his coffee while she helped herself to a cup.

"Do I smell biscuits?" she asked, trying to maintain the conversation alone. He shook his head.

"Croissants."

"*That's* what you were doing in here last night. Now I am impressed."

"Don't be," he told her tersely. "They were the frozen variety."

"Oh." She surmised from the word tense that there weren't any left.

"You'll find a couple more in the freezer," he said, confirming her supposition. He gathered his cap and gloves into one hand and walked to the sink, where he put his cup down. "Well, I'm off."

"Owen!" She hadn't meant to sound so sharp, but it had the desired effect. He stopped on his way to the door and turned back, one brow raised skeptically. She felt color rise to her cheeks. "I, um, don't know how to get to the ski area."

"It's fairly simple," he said, and then he started to explain, but Bonnie shook her head.

"I'm lost already. How about if you write it down for me? Or better still, if you could wait just one minute, I'll change and . . . follow you."

She thought at first that he would refuse. His gaze, so green today that it was startling, dropped to his hands, and his jaw worked from side to side as if literally moving around the thoughts inside his head. Finally he looked up.

"Might as well ride out with me," he said. "No sense in taking two automobiles when we're both going to the same place."

She clapped her hands together once, but managed to curb the celebration before it became too overt. "I won't be a minute, I swear!" she exclaimed, and ran from the room.

She pulled off her sweater at the same moment she entered the bedroom. Frantically grabbing items from drawers, boxes, and closet, she assembled her gear. Within moments she had stripped down to her bra and panties and pulled on a pair of bright yellow insulating underwear with long sleeves and legs. Next went on sock liners and yellow socks, followed by a blue ski suit, which she zipped only to midchest. She stuffed sunscreen, glove liners, gloves, hairbrush, lipstick, slim goggles, and her wallet into a small yellow pouch that belted around her waist, then went out with her white, lightweight ski boots clipped together and tossed over her shoulder. From the ski rack in the entry closet she took her skis, and with boots on one shoulder and skis on the other, she negotiated her way through the dining room to the kitchen.

Without a word, Owen took the skis and carried them outside, allowing her the opportunity to step into her boots. The boots were the latest front entry model, easy to step into and out of and easier to walk in when unbuckled than the conventional sort. Bonnie had them on in no time and was outside even before he had the skis stowed away in the back of the truck. A moment later they were backing out of the drive in the pickup. Bonnie paid close attention to their route as Owen drove them through the cleared city streets and onto Highway 24, heading west and north toward the slopes at the ski area.

Bonnie could tell that they were gaining in altitude because she had begun to feel that dreaded pressure behind her face. By the time they reached the parking lot of the ski center, her head was aching, and she found that she was quite out of breath long before they had reached the lodge. To her dismay, Owen did not slow down but strode on ahead of her as if he had every intention of abandoning her. Disgusted with herself and angry with him, she stopped to lean against her skis and attempt to catch her breath. Before long she was able to go on, but by the time she stowed her skis and reached the lift ticket office, she was winded again.

"One," she told the cashier breathlessly, but the pretty blonde only smiled and leaned closer to the glass partition.

"Are you Bonnie, Owen's new partner?"

Partner? Just hearing her and Owen's names spoken in context with that word lifted her spirits.

"Bonnie Maxwell," she said, slipping her hand through the portal in the window. The woman took it gladly.

"Celia Zimmer. Pleased to meet you, Bonnie. Owen says you'll probably buy a season pass, but today's skiing is on us. Just attach this complimentary pass to a visible spot on your person and enjoy."

"Thanks." Bonnie passed the wire hanger through the eye of the zipper head on her breast pocket, peeled the dated label from the backing, and folded the label over the hanger, pressing the sticky side together. "Did Owen say where he'd be?" she asked.

"Inside, upstairs," came the reply.

Bonnie smiled and pulled open the door on her immediate left. A blast of warm air hit her as she stepped into the narrow hallway. The hallway flanked the stairwell and opened onto the nursery and the locker room, off of which opened the public rest rooms. Bonnie started the climb, her boots clomping awkwardly. When she reached the top, her head was pounding.

She looked around her. A shop was to her right. To her left was a large dining room flanked on one side by a service area and on another by a wall of large windows. Owen was sitting with a number of other people at a table in front of one of the windows. Before him sat a plate of scrambled eggs and bacon. As Bonnie walked toward them, two

of the men at the table got up. A third stayed seated, a cur-
vaceous redhead occupying his lap. Owen, too, got to his
feet.

"Bonnie, I want you to meet some friends of mine," he
said, beginning with the two men who had risen. "Kim
Nabob and Jack Hampton. The heavy breathers at the end
of the table are Anne and Martin Ferguson, newlyweds of
four years."

Everyone greeted her enthusiastically. Bonnie was
thrilled, not only at their attitudes but at Owen's. He actually seemed to accept her as one of the group. As she sat
down, he slid the plate of eggs in front of her and placed a
cup of coffee beside it.

"Eat your breakfast," he said. "I want to get on those
slopes, and these are for your headache." He fished a couple of aspirin from his pocket and put them in her hand.
She wanted to ask how he knew, but the smile on his face
and his relaxed, accepting manner left her staring in wonder. Several moments passed before she could get herself
together, and by then the talk among the friends had
resumed.

The conversation was light and easy. Bonnie learned,
among other things, that the day's skiers would consist almost entirely of local folk who couldn't resist the combination of snow and sunshine, that it would be more
crowded later in the day, and that everyone in town was
waiting for Owen to open a restaurant.

"His buffalo brisket is the stuff of legends," Kim told
her. Bonnie could only raise her eyebrows.

"Buffalo?"

"Quail," Anne Ferguson put in. "Roast quail has got to
be his specialty. He made quail for us on our last anniver-
sary, and it was the highlight of the evening."

"Well, not the highlight," her husband amended, giving her rump a pat, "close, but not the highlight." Everyone laughed. Owen just shook his head.

Bonnie cleaned up her plate and swallowed the aspirin, even though her headache had already receded significantly. The group rose as one and moved out onto the deck that was built against the slope of the mountain. There were tables here, also, and skiers were claiming them with bags of gear. Many families were there, some with children as young as three strapped on their own skis. Bonnie found that Owen, Kim, and Jack had all stowed their skis in the same rack as she had, so they all went to get outfitted together, arranging to meet the Fergusons at the chair lift.

Ten minutes later, Bonnie and her three escorts were making their way to the chair lift, where the Fergusons waited. Everyone fell into line. Anne and Martin took the first chair. Kim and Jack took the second, and Owen and Bonnie just naturally claimed the third. As their feet swung free of the ground, the lift bore them steadily upward and over the treetops. Skis dangled, and a vista of green and white beauty unfolded before them.

"This is great," Bonnie said. "It's not crowded, and the slopes are clear. And your friends are very nice."

Owen nodded. "They're a good bunch."

"Thanks for bringing me along," she said.

He shrugged, the nylon of his coat swishing as his shoulders moved beneath it. "Glad to."

She sent him a look of frank surprise. "Does this mean you don't hate me anymore?"

His mouth dropped open. "What made you think I ever hated you?"

"You did."

He was clearly astounded. "Bonnie, honey," he said, his blue-green eyes holding hers, "I have a lot of ambivalent feelings about this partnership, but I certainly have never hated you. In fact, part of the problem is that I like you far too much.''

Bonnie's chest swelled with a sudden intake of breath. He liked her *too much?* Suddenly she knew what the problem with that kiss was, the problem with everything. It was *too much* for Owen Ketter, *too much* for a man who had already been burned by *too much* intense feeling for the wrong woman. He was scared. It wasn't that he wouldn't let himself like her but that he couldn't keep himself from it. Bonnie scared the hell out of Owen Ketter—and she couldn't have been happier about it.

Chapter Five

The lift approached the furrowed snow in a gentle slide. Owen gathered his poles into one hand, slid forward onto the edge of the seat, and tilted his skis, heels down. Beside him, Bonnie was doing the same. His skis met the slope. The chair carried him smoothly to the top of the incline. He shifted his weight to his feet, and the chair turned away, continuing its interminable journey. Owen glided easily downward, Bonnie beside him. They turned and dug in, then sidestepped quickly to clear the way for those following them. Owen took a minute to let Bonnie look around her.

They were halfway up the mountain. A wide, level area had been cut into the slope. A pair of deep impressions shaped like bowls had been dug into the level area, and several skiers were even then spiraling downward toward the bottom. Other than a couple of huts and a series of signs and a fringe of trees, there was nothing but snow and a handful of skiers.

"Follow me," Owen said, and Bonnie nodded before setting her goggles over her eyes. Her smile was bright, her dark hair sleek and shiny. She was too lovely to look at, like the sun. Owen looked away and pushed off, feeling light and happy and at peace, and why not? He loved to ski. The slopes were all but deserted. The snow was deep. The air was clear and as brilliant as fine crystal. And there was Bonnie.

She was dangerous, and he knew it, precisely because he liked her too much, but he didn't know how to stop the pleasure that filled him when she walked into the room. He chose an intermediate slope simply because it was the prettiest trail and started an easy descent, gliding smoothly side to side. Bonnie adapted quickly, her trail crisscrossing his. He found himself laughing as she skied into view time and time again. Just the sight of her was enough to make him feel giddy, and he wasn't the only one.

Steve Clark had a real case on Bonnie. He looked at her like a hungry kid looked at a piece of candy. Owen wanted to bust his chops, but he wouldn't. He had no right, and he didn't intend to have the right. Ever. Not if it meant giving Bonnie or any woman the power he'd given Tish, the power to break his heart, to crush him, to take away his will to achieve, to live. Yet, he remembered how it had been when Bonnie had stepped up into the concession area. Both Kim and Jack had openly ogled. Even Martin, his Anne in his lap, had taken a long, avid look. His own heart had swelled with pride simply because that stunning woman was with him. He had let them think she was his. Anne had said, "Owen, you sly dog," and Kim had said, "More like a lucky dog, if you ask me," and Owen had just smiled, his eyes on that tall, slender body coming his way. He'd felt her pleasure as he'd offered her breakfast, and the guilt he'd felt for not having done so earlier had vanished, as had the cloud of gloom that had hung over him since he'd kissed her.

He promised himself he wouldn't do that again. That kiss had rocked him right down to the soles of his feet. It had put ideas in his head, dangerous ideas. It had made him think of loving her, not only then but many times since. Sometimes it seemed that he thought of nothing else, and he knew that if he was to keep his heart he must keep his distance from her, but today was different somehow. Today felt "safe."

Owen looked down the mountain and saw Anne and Martin snowplowing to let them catch up. A moment later, Jack came zooming by, followed immediately by Kim, who made a wave at Bonnie, lost it, and tumbled. He was up in an instant, and Bonnie laughed as they passed him. He brushed snow from his shoulders and reattached a ski, then came down in a fast crouch to issue a challenge. Suddenly it was a race, all six of them flying, and then it was no race at all as Bonnie tucked and leveled, a flash of blue and long black hair that left everyone behind.

Kim whooped, blown away by the effortless grace of obvious skill and style. Jack screamed out the words, "Speed Demon!" Owen, Martin, and Anne came to stops. Anne shook her poles in the air and celebrated the victory of one of her own sex, then shoved off again as Bonnie sent up a wave of snow as she came to a halt. Martin pushed up his goggles and sent Owen a knowing look.

"Damn," he said, "she's something. And just when I was sure you'd sworn off. Where'd you find her, anyway?"

Owen lifted his head to look downhill where Anne and Bonnie were pelting Kim and Jack with snow. "You might say she found me."

Martin laughed and clapped his big friend on the shoulder, his pole dangling from his wrist by a strap. "I should have known you wouldn't go looking for it."

It? Owen thought. And what was it? Sex? Love? He bowed his head, knowing this was the moment to disabuse Martin of erroneous assumptions, and cleared his throat. "*It* isn't what you think."

"Oh?" Martin was dubious.

"It's pretty much business."

"That's lust for a buck I see on your face, eh?"

Owen felt himself flush. "You know, Marty, not every man thinks with his crotch," he countered defensively.

Martin just grinned. "You're no monk, big guy, and even if you were, that little temptation down there could make you rethink."

Owen just glowered and shoved off, Martin's laughter following him down, that of the others rising to meet him. As he drew near, the four snowballers broke off their game, Bonnie moving naturally toward him. He snubbed her. He knew it was mean and childish and inappropriate, but he didn't know how else to counter what he was so obviously feeling for her. Without so much as a word or a glance, he poled straight past her toward the western slope and the three-man lift that would take them to the top of the mountain. He could feel her confusion, and a part of him went out to her, but he told himself it was more cruel to lead her on. Wasn't it?

The rest of the party followed him to the second lift, somewhat subdued by the sudden change in his demeanor. He caught the first chair alone, disliking himself and everyone else, but he shortly heard laughter behind him, Bonnie's voice ringing clear and light above the others, and he felt a little better. He dismounted at the top and chose a black trail for himself, starting a fast, fierce descent that required all of his concentration. He flew over the moguls, landing in perfect squats and skimming the powder with breakneck speed. He seemed to have the trail all to himself and felt it was just as well, for he needed this time to get himself in hand. He needed the all-consuming involvement of fast, dangerous physical exertion, and that's exactly what he got. There were moments when he scared himself, careening too close to a tree or taking a jump at a dangerous cant or veering into deep powder that sprayed over the tops of his boots and threatened to topple him, but he pushed on, taking a forty-five-minute course in just under thirty-three. When he reached the bottom, he was exhausted but exhilarated, turning to a stop that fanned snow in a wide arc and slumping over his skis, panting.

"Bet you can't do it again." He looked up to find Bonnie, his surprise evident. "We took a little blue," she said. "I told the others I never ski the challenge slope first time down. Then I told them how wrong they were about us."

He straightened and pushed up his goggles, his blue-green eyes studying her. "Did you?"

"Um-hm. I said we were business partners and friends and nothing more." His brows went up in tandem. "Well, it's the truth, isn't it? I mean, we are friends?"

He didn't know why that made him smile, but he felt his mouth curving up with surprising ease. "Maybe we are at that." She beamed.

"Okay. So, friend to friend, I bet I can beat you down that black slope by a mile."

"Oh, do you now?"

She was grinning. "Unless you're too tired to give me a chance."

"I'll rest on the lift."

"Maybe you ought to get a little rest right now," she said, reaching out with both hands. "Why don't you lie down for a while?'' And the next thing he knew he was falling backward.

Owen flailed at the air, lost both skis, and hit the ground. His initial reaction was shock, then outrage, then suddenly amusement.

"Last one down's a loser!" she teased, laughing. He took a harmless swipe at her, and she jerked back, pushing off toward the lift. Feeling a devilish sense of challenge, he got himself up and back onto his skis, then went after her.

She was already on the lift by the time he reached it, but he didn't let that deter him. Making his excuses, he pushed to the front of the line and caught the fourth chair to follow her. At the first stop, she hopped down, gave him a wave and started her run. He hurried after her, but when he reached the halfway mark, she was long gone. Then he heard her laughter and looked up to spy her riding the three-man alone against the western sky.

"Damn!" He put his head down and poled doggedly toward the lift.

She was waiting at the top of the black trail, and the sight of her smile broadened his own.

"All right, hotshot," he said. "We already know who's the cutest. Now we'll see who's the fastest." He took a firm hold on his poles and shouted, "Go!"

For the first several moments it was neck-and-neck, but that first mogul put her yards ahead of him. She jumped and practically sailed the rest of the way. He couldn't believe it, and was, in fact, so enthralled by the mere sight of her that he couldn't concentrate on his own performance. He made himself push, but when he reached the bottom, she was already out of her skis and gathering them into her hands. She straightened, breathing hard and grinning, her goggles pushed up into her hair. He ripped off his gloves and pulled down his own goggles so he could get a good look at her.

"Who taught you to ski?" he wanted to know.

She shrugged. "Some blond guy named Thor."

Thor. That figured. "All right, hotshot," he said, puffing. "So we know who's cutest *and* fastest. Don't let it go to your head. Now, if you'll tell me where I can find this Thor, I'd like to go and break his legs."

She laughed, shouldering her skis. "Save your energy. I hear some jealous husband already did that."

For some reason, that news didn't exactly please him, but he put aside the feeling, took off his skis, and trudged along behind her as she made her way to the concession building.

None of their group was inside, so Bonnie bought him a cup of coffee, and they sat down to rest awhile. Soon the others came in, talking and laughing. They gathered around the table, teasing and telling absurd stories. Owen felt at ease with Bonnie at his side, despite his misgivings, and when he realized she wasn't going to tell how she'd beat him down the black slope, he did so himself. He took a good bit of ribbing—from everyone but Bonnie, which he found oddly endearing. God knew Tish had never passed up a single opportunity to humiliate him. That woman honestly hadn't seemed to understand that he had feelings and that she could hurt them. For the first time, the thought of Tish did not make him want to push Bonnie away.

They made another run before lunch, the whole group, and afterward Owen went into the kitchen to prepare beer soup and Reuben sandwiches for everyone. Bonnie couldn't believe the concession just let him wander around the place and make his own lunch, using whatever ingredients he could find, not even when the others told her he did it nearly everywhere he went. But then, sometimes Owen didn't believe it himself, despite the fact that it seemed natural for him to be in the kitchen. Like it seemed natural for him to be with Bonnie? The thought both unnerved and calmed him. He could feel himself moving closer to her, but somehow he didn't feel as threatened as before. He chalked it up to the day and the weather and the company of good friends and the exhilaration of skiing and good food and everything else he could think of, everything and everyone but Bonnie herself.

After lunch, for which he received the usual kudos, he went out to the truck and got his snowboard. To his delight, Bonnie was avid to try it, and he had no doubt that she would be an excellent "snow surfer." He started her on an easy green slope and by midafternoon was regretting it.

"You may never get to use that board again!" Jack told him. "Unless you buy her one of her own."

The idea made Owen grin, but he instantly suppressed it. He had no business buying her anything, none whatsoever, especially as he didn't have the money. He needed to be putting every cent into the lodge—unless he wanted a partner permanently. For the first time he turned that idea over in his head. It wouldn't be so bad really. It'd give him a little disposable income for a change, someone with whom to share the work load. *And an involvement you can't handle,* he reminded himself, because not even he could believe he was able to spend an indefinite amount of time with her without giving in to his desires. No, it wouldn't work, but Bonnie had a way of making him wish it would.

They stayed until the slopes closed around four o'clock, then drove into town as a group to have drinks before going their separate ways. It was a companionable, happy time. Bonnie seemed to be as much a part of the gang as any of them. The guys were certainly accepting of her, and Anne was thrilled to have found another female with whom to buddy around.

Anne was the best woman Owen knew, as enamored of Martin as Martin was of her. In addition, she was as fun and bright and frank as Bonnie herself—and almost as attractive. Yet Owen had never envied Martin. His own experience with love had taught him that it was a chancy business at best and apt to change from one instant to another. The way he saw it, both Martin and Anne were taking a chance. They just didn't know how big a chance it was, and he hoped they never found out. As for him, he already knew love wasn't worth the risk, for as grand as love was, the pain of losing it was worse, and he had no intention of ever letting himself forget that.

Nevertheless, when Bonnie slid into the booth at the local tavern, he found himself sliding in next to her, and with Kim sitting on the outside, it was a tight fit indeed, so tight he had to lift up his arm and drape it around her shoulders in order to make room to maneuver. She didn't seem to mind. In fact, she didn't even seem to notice, and so he put it out of his mind and joined in the conversation. He put it so far out of mind that when Kim got up to leave, he didn't even think of moving over. He didn't think of it when Jack left either, or when Martin got up to go feed quarters into the jukebox, or even when Anne excused herself to go to the ladies' room. He didn't think of it until they were alone and Bonnie turned to look at him, her pale gray eyes as soft as clouds. Then suddenly he couldn't think of anything else except how perfectly she fitted against him, hip to hip, her long, slender thigh pressed to his, her shoulder tucked up under his arm. It was the last thing he wanted to do, but he made himself move away and pulled in his arm, leaning forward on his elbows against the tabletop. She smiled a gentle smile that held nothing of censure.

"They're such nice people," she said. "Everyone I've met here is so nice, especially you."

He frowned into his highball glass, not only because she'd said it, but because it wasn't true. He'd been anything but nice to her at times, and he longed to tell her that he'd acted that way in self-defense, but he didn't dare. Instead, he shrugged.

"Nice people get treated nice," he said, and she laughed softly, reaching for her wineglass.

"Thanks. But I have every reason to be nice. You don't."

He let himself look at her. "Why do you say that?"

Her light gray gaze was frank. "Because I was forced on you," she said. "You didn't ask me to come here. You have to share your business with me, your home, your life. Even a nice man would prove testy under similar circumstances. And you're so much more than just a nice man."

He couldn't believe she had said that. He hadn't been nice to her. He had been downright hostile at times. She was the one who seemed determined to be nice no matter what he said or did. He thought of telling her that, but he'd never been good at talking to women. In the end, he merely shook his head and looked down at his hands. "This was a good day," he said finally, hoping to change the subject. It didn't work.

"Yes, it was," she answered softly. "It proved to me that there's a pretty great guy under all that pain." He was truly stunned, and so was she. "Didn't you think I could tell?" she asked, her head canted to one side. "That you are in pain, I mean."

He was appalled. "You . . . you don't know what you're talking about."

"Don't I?" she asked softly, and her hand lifted to his arm, sliding along the inside to the bend of his elbow, where it settled.

He was trembling. If just the look of her, just that little touch, could make him tremble, what would it be like to hold her against him, naked, panting? But no. No way. He didn't need that kind of trouble. He shook his head to clear it, instinctively tensing his muscles to control the tremor. She removed her hand, moving it to the nape of her neck, fingers sliding beneath the thick, straight mass of her hair.

He knew he should say something soothing, but he didn't know what it should be. Absently, he turned his glass upon its napkin, trying to formulate words, but all he could do was wonder how she knew. Was he so obvious, or was it her, some special sense like ESP? Did she know what he was thinking, feeling, now? Could she look at him and tell that he wanted to put his arms around her and hold her to him like a kid with a security blanket?

Fortunately Anne returned to the table then. Owen fastened his attention on her gratefully. She said something, and he laughed, hoping it was clever. Apparently it was, for she sent him a pleased look and began to prattle. He had never felt such relief, but beneath it was the ache, that deep, fearful yearning that scared the hell out of him. Did Bonnie know? Could she tell? He was terrified that she would see and reach out to him. What would he do then? How could he resist? She would touch his body, and he would be lost, seeking that feeling of completion that came with sated desire. He was trembling again, and he didn't know what to do about it. If only she wasn't so sweet, so understanding, so eager to please, if only she wasn't beautiful and bright and attentive, if only she didn't try so hard to do and say the right thing, maybe he could protect himself, harden himself against her, drive her away. He had to find a way to do that. God knew he didn't want to hurt her, but he had to find a way to protect himself. He had to.

*   *   *

It started with the television set. Buoyed by that lovely day they'd spent skiing together, and bothered by the bored sighs of their few guests in that following week, Bonnie had asked him if it wouldn't be a good idea to get a better television set into the recreation room, and after one of those interminable discussions where she did most of the talking while he mainly stared, he had surprised her by agreeing. She had been so delighted that she hadn't bothered with details. She'd simply set out to explore the offerings of the local merchants, found what she wanted, bought it, and had it delivered to the house. It had all seemed so wonderfully easy, but she was learning that with Owen Ketter nothing was ever easy. With Owen one must *always* sweat the details. She knew the moment he laid eyes on it that there would be trouble, and now he stood glaring at her as if he'd only then discovered she'd stolen the thing.

"That's not a TV," he said, his voice lifting to a yell. "That's a movie screen!" His arms flew out in different directions, making her flinch. "How on earth can you call that thing a television?"

"But it's what everyone is buying now," she told him, trying to remain calm, trying to explain. "I really didn't think about buying anything else."

"Oh, no, you wouldn't!" he retorted. "Little Miss Moneybags *never* thinks about what she buys! She just goes straight to the most expensive one and says, 'I'll take that.'"

She was wounded. It simply wasn't true. There were less expensive sets, to be sure, but more expensive ones as well. She'd chosen this one because it was the best bargain, the best value for the dollar. It was unfair of him to say she hadn't shopped responsibly.

"I only did what I thought was best," she argued, but he was clearly beyond listening.

"And what the hell is this?" He was looking at the controls. "A VCR?"

"It's built-in," she pointed out doggedly. "That's one reason it's such a good buy."

"And I suppose the video game system was a good buy, too?" He was practically sneering at her.

She stiffened, trying to tamp down her rising anger. "It was part of the deal. The salesman threw it in as an inducement."

"I'll bet he did," he came back caustically. "He knew a big spender when he saw one."

She threw her shoulders back, annoyed now as well as angry. "Do you act like this with everyone who has more money than you?" she asked snidely.

He was gathering himself up for a real explosion when the front door opened upstairs and footsteps carried someone in. From the sound of it, one of their guests had returned from a short day of less than great skiing, an unlikely spurt of warmish weather having turned the powder into slush on the slopes. They heard the clacking sounds of skis bumping together or against other objects, the thumping of overshoes falling by the wayside, the muted clump of footsteps softened by rubber soles. Then a pair of sneakers appeared on the top rung of the stairway and descended step by lagging step, displaying a growing length of red-suited leg. Owen scowled at Bonnie and swallowed whatever it was he'd been about to say, then moved swiftly to the staircase and bounded up it, brushing by the descending interrupter.

"Hello, Mr. Ketter." Bonnie recognized the voice of Larry Carpenter, a rather sadly competent young man from Corpus Christi. He was the sort of fellow often labeled as a nerd, which may have accounted for the fact that he was traveling alone. He struck her as being hopelessly out of place in a city like Corpus Christi, the proverbial ninety-pound weakling apt to have sand kicked in his face on the beach. He was also determinedly good-natured, and she knew the fact that Owen had not returned his greeting would not deter him. She tried to make herself cheerful as he gained the lower floor and turned to find her. "Hello, Miss Max— Wow!" His attention went instantly to the big screen television now occupying one wall.

"That's Max*well*," Bonnie teased, but he didn't get it. "Huh?"

"Never mind." She gave him a smile. Larry Carpenter always struck her as the sort of person who was constantly in need of a smile. He beamed at her, then walked over to the television, taking a careful inventory.

"Do you have games for this?" he asked eagerly, holding up one of the control pads. Bonnie shook her head.

"No, I don't, but I understand they rent them at the video rental outlet, and I've opened an account for the lodge there. Just tell them you're a guest."

"Great!" He moved toward his room, then halted and said a very funny thing. "This is big on the list, Miss Maxwell, very big indeed!"

She didn't have time to ask him what list that would be, for he quickly exited. What an odd little man he was. He'd actually asked for the worst room in the place when he'd booked his visit, not the cheapest, but the worst. She shook her head. Men. What rational being could comprehend them?

She kept out of Owen's way the remainder of that day, then girded herself for an unpleasant dinner, despite the delicious aroma of brisket barbecuing in the oven. She need not have bothered, however, because Owen no longer seemed spoiling for a fight. Oh, he was angry, but he didn't seem anxious to talk about it, which wasn't so surprising really. It was, in fact, very much in character. Bonnie let it alone, hoping the argument would die a gentle, natural death, and concentrated instead on serving the half-dozen or so guests who had wandered in from the slopes.

Everyone was rather subdued because of the disappointing skiing conditions, everyone but Larry Carpenter, who seemed about to burst with some delightful secret. Bonnie had seated the fellow next to herself simply because he had not appeared to make friends with the others and she didn't like to see him eating alone, but his unusual smugness was an irritation this particular evening, especially when he kept alluding to "what he was about to do for her." The meal was nearly over by the time he came out with it, and a very dramatic presentation he made of it, too. He waited until everyone had fallen silent, intent upon their food, then with carefully calculated importance leaned upon his elbow, bringing his head near hers, and cleared his throat. Bonnie sent him an exasperated look, which he merely ignored, so delighted was he with his news.

"I have something I want to say," he announced needlessly, thin lips drawing thinner still in a grimace of a smile. Bonnie was aware of Owen's sudden interest, but Carpenter had laid his hand on her arm, and she felt it would be rude to look away. "Now, I know the skiing hasn't been great," Larry Carpenter began, "but it's early in the season and all the projections are good for the peak, so even though I'm leaving early, I don't want you to be concerned. I'm going to recommend you. The accommodation, I mean." He sat back and folded his arms, as if this news was of immense proportions.

Bonnie smiled and turned her attention back to her plate. "That's very nice," she said.

Whether because of her lack of enthusiasm or despite it, Carpenter leaned forward and addressed himself to Owen. "It's the new entertainment that's done it," he divulged with a nod of his head. "My group is mad for anything video—games, movies, anything. It's the wave of the future, you know, home video."

Bonnie looked at Owen, and Owen looked at Bonnie. *The wave of the future?* she thought. *How about the wave of the now?*

Owen seemed to be thinking along those same lines. He put down his fork and engaged Carpenter politely. "I'm afraid you've lost me. What's this about video?"

Carpenter threw up his soft, pale hands. "The entertainment center, man! In the recreation room."

Owen looked at Bonnie, and Bonnie smiled. "Do you mean the new television set, Mr. Carpenter?" she chirped, glad for once to see Owen's glower.

"Television, shmelevision!" Carpenter declared. "That, my lady, is entertainment! It's exactly the sort of thing we look for."

"We?" Owen asked in a slightly strangled voice.

"My club!" Owen proclaimed, immediately holding back their questions with an uplifted hand. "I'm the advance man," he went on. "Purely incognito, you understand. And what better way to check out the facilities? There's more to life than sun and sea, you know, and it's upon that premise that the Intellectual Fun Club is founded. We're committed to broadening our minds through a wide variety of experience and entertainment, and that's why we love video. The computer-aided home video system is the harbinger of future intellectual fun! Soon one won't even have to leave the comfort of home to experience the thrill of skiing. And think of it! It won't matter what the weather's like! On video, it's always perfect! For now, however, we'll simply have to settle for the real thing, skiing, that is. But at least here we have the state-of-the-art gamesmanship equipment to fill the remaining hours! Oh, and the other suggestions you made were quite good, too, Miss Maxwell.''

Again Bonnie found herself smiling, but Owen's look was more one of desperation. ''I'm almost afraid to ask,'' he said, gazing at Bonnie.

She shrugged. ''I just told Mr. Carpenter what type of activities are available in Leadville beyond skiing.''

''But it's that fine new equipment you've installed downstairs that's decided me,'' he volunteered.

''Decided you?'' Owen inquired gently.

''To recommend your accommodation to the club!''

''Ah.'' Owen bowed his head. ''And how many are there in your club, Mr. Carpenter?''

''Twenty-five.'' Bonnie laughed aloud, and Owen squeezed his eyes shut. ''But I wouldn't count on more than eighteen or nineteen reservations,'' Carpenter went on. ''We have our share of deadheads, if you know what I mean.''

''I do indeed,'' Owen said with a sigh. ''So have we, and I'm it.''

''Beg pardon?'' Carpenter's brows drew together. Bonnie leaned forward and patted his wrist with her long, nimble fingers.

''It's Owen's way of saying he was wrong about something,'' she told him quietly. ''But never mind. We look forward to seeing you again, Mr. Carpenter, and your friends, too. Perhaps we could arrange a little tournament of sorts for them, if you could suggest a suitably intellectual game....''

He clapped both hands onto the table. ''What a marvelous idea! I'll take a poll, see what's most popular. It's probably my personal favorite, Pac-Man, but one wants to be certain.''

Bonnie could only smile. To say what she was thinking would have been not only rude, but disastrous. Carpenter pushed away his plate and got up, so apparently intrigued by this new idea that he could no longer concentrate on his meal. Bonnie held her laughter until he was safely out of earshot and then only dared snigger.

"Intellectual game, my eye!" Owen groused. "Wave of the future! That nitwit wouldn't know a wave of the future if it washed right over him."

"I wouldn't be too sure," Bonnie cautioned good-naturedly. "Listen."

Sure enough, those guests who had already finished their dinners and gone down to the recreation room were playing a rented video game on the new system. The pings and pows and sputters were unmistakable. Owen sighed.

"Mea culpa," he muttered. "You win, but don't you dare say you told me so."

"I wouldn't dream of it," Bonnie assured him sincerely. But there was another matter that came to mind, one they had broached before, and she was determined to bring it up again. Perhaps the moment was at hand. With carefully chosen words, she might be able to build a great success on one little victory after another. She put her chin onto her palm and smiled. It was just a matter of time, after all, before he realized she was right.

Chapter Six

The phone rang, but before Bonnie could get up off the step, it stopped. Owen was home. The idea made her polish this last spindle a little more vigorously, the oil on her dust rag coaxing a warm luster from the red-brown wood. Dusting was not her favorite activity, but there was a certain satisfaction to be had from a staircase bordered on both sides by shiny hand-turned spindles. As she sat back and surveyed her handiwork, however, she was truly thankful that Owen had had the good sense to paint the top rail. It was much easier to wash away hand prints than to polish them away. She only hoped Owen had as much good sense when it came to economic issues.

But of course he had. His business experience was extensive. The only reason he hadn't done some of the things she proposed was because of his serious lack of capital. He'd solved that problem by taking her on as a partner. *A smart move, if I do say so myself,* she mused. The best part was that he seemed to be thinking the same way lately, ever since the Intellectual Fun Club of Houston had booked accommodation for twenty later in the season. *So why are you waiting?* she asked herself, as if she didn't know.

It was nearly Thanksgiving, for Pete's sake, and still she hadn't approached Owen about the advertising campaign she had in mind. Harv was right when he said it was essential to her success here, and he said it often enough over the phone. Besides, there was no reason for this delay. Everything was ready. She had all the estimates she needed and a well-reasoned program laid out. The money was sitting in their joint business account just waiting to be used, and she even had her contacts in Texas lined up. All she needed was Owen's permission to go ahead. So why hadn't she asked?

It was simple really. She just didn't want to upset the applecart. They were friends now, and it was so nice to just be pleasant to one another, to come downstairs in the morning and be greeted with a cup of coffee and a smile, to chat over dinner about such wide-ranging topics as snowboarding and old movies and books, music, family, politics. She knew, however, that the cost of this advertising project was going to be a problem for Owen, and she dreaded the showdown. Something told her this argument would not be an easy one to win. But it wasn't going to get any easier, either, so it might as well be now.

She got up from her seat on the bottom step and gathered the cleaning things scattered about the foyer. What she hadn't scrubbed, polished, swept, vacuumed, or waxed that day, she'd thrown into the washer and dryer, and now she had a mountain of linens to fold, some of them quite threadbare, but otherwise her chores were done. The house was clean, as a glance or a sniff would attest, and Owen was back from picking up those things at the grocery store that their regular suppliers could not deliver. It was time. Quickly, before her courage could dwindle, she stowed her cleaning gear in the so-called maintenance closet beneath the stairwell, tugged the scarf off her head, and fluffed and smoothed her hair with her hands. Her jeans and sweat-shirt were dusty and spotted with oil, as were her athletic shoes, but then she wasn't trying to seduce the man, just convince him to let her spend a little money on an adver-tising campaign, and it wouldn't hurt to remind him how well she was performing her other duties.

She walked through the dining room into the kitchen, then, failing to find him there, on into the back hallway and down its length to the door at its end. It was open. She knocked on the door frame and stuck her head inside. He was standing at his desk, the telephone receiver pressed be-tween shoulder and ear as he wrote with a pencil on a large desk calendar.

"Okay," he was saying, "that's five extra guests, the two females will be staying with the two already scheduled, which means they'll need a double instead of a single. The three guys can go into the dormitory, leaving room for two more. You sure you don't want to go ahead and book that space, too?"

Bonnie folded her arms and lounged in the doorway, waiting. He said his goodbyes and hung up, turning before the receiver had even made contact with the cradle.

"The Intellectual Fun Club of Corpus Christi?" Bonnie asked.

He grinned. "You don't suppose they're all like Larry Carpenter, do you? Because if they are, it's going to look like a geek convention around here."

She furrowed her brow as if in deep thought. "Can't be," she concluded. "Corpus Christi doesn't have twenty-five geeks."

He laughed. "Spoken like a true Texan."

It was her turn, but she couldn't think of any more clever repartee. She stalled, her gaze going around the room. She'd cleaned in here only a couple of hours earlier, vacuuming the deep, rust-colored carpet, dusting the pickled pine dresser and the painted desk, washing the three undraped windows that looked out over the backyard and the gazebo in its midst, changing the linens on that rickety four-poster bed. She figured Owen slept diagonally in that bed. It was the only way she could see him fitting into it, and she couldn't see him sharing it at all. No way could Owen and another person sleep in that bed at the same time. Of course, if their interest was in something other than sleep, she supposed they could maneuver between the foot- and headboards, but it seemed unlikely, and that pleased her. If Owen Ketter had enjoyed a woman's body since he'd come to Leadville, it hadn't been in that bed. *Not that it has anything to do with anything,* she told herself.

She realized she was staring at the bed and looked away, keeping her gaze level and unhurried. "You, um, really ought to drape those windows," she told him. "The room would be warmer."

"It's warm enough," he said lightly, and leaned against the edge of the desk. "Actually, what I ought to do is set up a real office, you know, someplace where we can both have access. I was thinking of dividing the mudroom, maybe, or one of the bigger bedrooms on this floor. What do you think?"

It was the perfect opening, and she made up her mind to take it. She realized she was trembling and breathed in deeply. "I think there are better places to put our money," she began. "For instance, I have this friend in Texas who says that a good color brochure in the right hands could more than double—"

"No way."

The interruption was all the more effective for its quiet delivery. Bonnie closed her mouth and swallowed. "Owen," she began again, "I think I've proved myself in the short time I've been here. I mean, I haven't been a total washout, have I?"

He folded his arms. "Your instincts have been right on target," he admitted, "and I'm sure they are this time, but that's beside the point."

She couldn't believe it. "You know I'm right, and you're still against it?"

"Bonnie, we're talking about photographers and a four-color printing process, not to mention the writing and the layout and the proofing and half a dozen other expenses."

"Two or three thousand dollars," she said. "It's a pittance! It's—"

"Out of the question," he finished for her.

The tone of his voice was reasonable. His face was not contorted in anger. Yet she had the feeling he had never been more determined. It struck her then how impotent she was. After everything she'd done, she was still hanging on here by her fingernails. She felt like crying, and that made her mad. She hated weepy females, detested them.

"You're so afraid I'm going to take over here!" she said, rushing on though he was shaking his head. "That's not what I want. That's not what partnership is about. I just want to help you make this place a success. What's wrong with that?"

"Nothing, but I told you in the beginning that I wouldn't have you investing more than I could reasonably pay back."

"Two or three thousand dollars!"

"Who do you think you're kidding?" he suddenly demanded, lunging onto his feet. "We're talking twice that, and it's only the beginning! Oh, no. I draw the line at turning my rec room into a video palace!''

Her mouth dropped open. "Why, you ungrateful, hypocritical, insecure—"

"Watch it!"

"Overgrown—"

"Bonnie!"

"Dropout!"

"That's it!"

He started forward, but she brought her hands to her hips, feet braced wide apart, just daring him to touch her. She was truly angry, blazingly so, and she tossed her head, glaring a challenge, her long hair swinging past her shoulders.

"We have twenty-five reservations in that book because I had the good sense to bring in that video equipment," she pointed out.

"If you had good sense," he told her in a low, rumbling voice, "you'd get the hell out of here as fast as humanly possible. In fact, I think that's just what you ought to do. Now."

She lifted her chin, thinking he was right, but in that same instant she knew she'd do anything to stay. Her anger vanished. Regret and fear rushed in. "You can't mean that. You promised me six months, and it's not even Thanksgiving yet."

He looked away, and she saw that his own anger was nothing more than a thin veneer for whatever else it was that he felt. He shook his head. "Bonnie, this has been a mistake, and we both know it. I never should have promised you those six months, and I can't justify letting you stay on here and work like a scrubwoman any longer."

"You promised me a chance," she reminded him, chagrined to hear her voice tremble.

"And at the same time I told you that I don't want a partner," he came back.

She was desperate, and desperation was a poor prompter. "If it doesn't work, you don't have to pay me back," she said quickly. "I don't care about the money. I care about making this work, and it's worth the risk of a little capital. It's worth—"

"For God's sake, Bonnie!" he snapped, and she flinched, her hands coming together at her waist. "What do I have to do to make you understand? I don't want a partner!"

"But you need one!" she protested.

"That's not the point!"

"You promised!" she screamed at him, her voice so shrill she lifted a hand to her mouth. Tears filled her eyes. She fought them back, head high, hand going down to her side. "You promised," she repeated reasonably, hurrying on when he opened his mouth to reply, "and I agreed to certain stipulations. I swore I wouldn't spend more money trying to make this place succeed than you could reasonably pay back if the partnership failed."

"When," he said in a gravelly voice, "*when* the partnership failed."

She lifted her chin a fraction of an inch higher. "If."

He stared at her a long moment, and then the corner of his mouth quirked and he looked away, clearing his throat. "I believe we were of two minds about this at the time," he said, "but you're right about the agreement."

She nodded. "And you're right about the cost of advertising. It's too much. Let's forget it."

His dark brows rose in tandem. "What?" He actually chuckled. "I don't believe it," he said, "I've actually won one."

She was so relieved at the bantering tone that it was easy to laugh. "Well, you were right for once. It's just that I know so many people back home in Texas who love to ski, and they're just so eager to hear about every new slope that opens up."

"Write a letter," he said drolly. "I'll give you a stamp."

"All right, all right. It's forgotten. Let's talk about something else."

"Such as?"

She shrugged. "Thanksgiving?"

"Oh, yeah," he said, snapping his fingers, "I meant to tell you, I took a booking from this couple named Scrivner. It seems they lost their son a few weeks ago, and somebody told them this was a quiet place, so they thought they'd spend the holidays here instead of at home. I told them they'd probably have the place all to themselves and that I'd cook them up a special Thanksgiving dinner."

"That's very sweet of you."

"Yeah, well, you know, it's not too busy around here about then. In fact, to tell you the truth, I usually have my two brothers and their families up for the holidays."

"But not this year?" she asked.

He shook his head. Bonnie bit her lip, picturing a taciturn but well-meaning Owen alone at the table with a bereaved couple on Thanksgiving Day. He'd cook a feast, of course, and the three of them would sit there picking at their food and trying to smile. The idea physically pained her, and she made an instant decision.

"I guess it'll just be the four of us then," she commented mildly.

He looked surprised. "You're not going to Texas for Thanksgiving?"

"I hadn't intended to," she lied. "Why?"

He shrugged. "I just figured you'd spend the holiday with your family."

She struck a nonchalant pose. "We're not really into that kind of thing. I mean, it's no big deal."

"No turkey with all the trimmings?" he asked.

"Well, you know," she said, and it was the absolute truth, "the cook gets the day off so she can spend it with her family."

Owen rolled his eyes. "Poor little rich girl," he teased. "We'll have to give you a real Thanksgiving this year."

Bonnie smiled. It wasn't an advertising campaign but it was something, and Owen wouldn't be alone with that poor couple on what was meant to be a family holiday. They would be together, she and Owen, and that seemed right to her, so right she'd do or say just about anything to keep it that way. *Or do without just about anything,* she mused, thinking of the well-planned advertising campaign she'd so willingly abandoned. It was then that she knew this was much more than business, and that for her it always would be.

Imogene Scrivner was a small, wonderfully made woman in her early forties with pale skin and paler hair that laid against her pretty head like a smooth, glossy pelt. Her husband, Walker, was obviously the younger of the two, and just as obviously adored his trim, gutsy little wife. An automobile accident had taken the life of their teenage son that previous spring, but they were determined, as Imogene put it, to "go on living."

"We couldn't face the idea of Thanksgiving at home without him," Walker explained on the morning of their arrival, "so we thought we'd do something different, and we both love to ski."

They were lovely people, brave, intelligent, and likable,
very up-front about their personal tragedy and their feelings. Bonnie liked them instantly and wanted to make their
holiday special in order to defray the pain of their loss.
Owen seemed of the same mind. It turned out to be a lot of
fun. She and Owen put their heads together and came up
with a plan, then divided the responsibilities according to
their individual talents. The table fell into Bonnie's scope.
She bought some inexpensive linens and four place set-
tings of fine white, gold-edged china, gold-plated flatware, and crystal. She scrounged up some candle holders
and brought in some fresh flowers.

Because the slopes were open on Thanksgiving Day and
the Scrivners wanted to ski, they decided to serve their feast
at the dinner hour. That gave Owen all day to work his
magic, with Bonnie's help, which she was only too happy
to give. The Scrivners came in about three-thirty, saying
with smiles on their faces that they were famished and exhausted and frozen through. Bonnie took them hot spiced
tea and a little plate of crisp cookies. By that time the good
smells coming from Owen's kitchen had permeated the
whole house, sparking their appetites, and they devoured
the cookies on sight, laughing at their own greediness.

At about five o'clock Bonnie went up to dress for dinner. She showered and put on a royal blue jersey knit dress
that fell straight from the shoulder to the floor, skimming
her body lightly. It was slit on both sides from the hem to
the knee, showing a tantalizing length of bare leg. The long,
tapered sleeves hugged her wrist, setting off her hands, still
pretty despite all her hard work. The straight neckline was
too wide to allow her to wear a bra without showing the
straps, so she went without. She twisted back her glossy
hair at the sides, whisked on a little makeup, including dark
blue shadow in the creases of her eyelids, rosy blush, and a

sheer lipstick of rich, sparkling red, and clipped on dangly silver bead earrings. Her shoes were soft-soled flats of blue suede decorated with rhinestones the size of her thumbnail.

Owen's eyes popped when she walked into the kitchen. "Wow," he said, shaking his head slowly from side to side when she asked if it was too much. She thanked him with a smile and went out to "set the stage."

She pulled the smallest table into place in front of the dining room window, selected four matching chairs to accompany it, and went to work. First went on a plain white cloth, followed by a champagne-beige lace overlay. Next came the china, napkins, flatware, and crystal. She placed the candles on alternate corners of the table, and on either side of them arranged small bowls of fall flowers accented with beige paper bows, for a total of four bowls. This done, she filled the salt and pepper shakers, chilled the wine, turned on some soft music, lined up the serving dishes on the counter for Owen's convenience, prepared the dessert cart, filled the ice bucket, and mixed a small pitcher of the Scrivners' preferred drink, martinis, which she carried up to them with the news that dinner would be served in twenty minutes. When she returned to the dining room, she found that Owen had already brought in the turkey. It was browned to perfection and trickling the most wonderfully aromatic juices.

He came in ten minutes later wearing dark green pleated slacks and a matching turtleneck under a black jacket with a trim shawl collar. A dark green silk handkerchief peeked out of his breast pocket. His belt and the uppers of his shoes were made of woven black leather, and he was wearing an expensive gold watch that she'd never seen before. He was gorgeous with his vivid blue-green eyes and cleanly shaved golden skin and silvery hair waving back from his temples and falling forward rakishly over his dark brows. Bonnie's heart stopped at the sight of him, and she knew that she had never before seen a man the way she saw Owen Ketter. It was as if every cell of her body was instantly, keenly aware of him, as if that awareness filled even the pores of her skin and all the other empty spaces, small and large, that existed in her. She was so glad she'd stayed to share this time with him and had a hand in making it special. She only hoped he was feeling the same.

Owen looked at Bonnie standing there looking at him. She had the wine in her hands and was about to decant it, but for the moment she merely stared, her lush red lips parted slightly, pale eyes sparkling with an emotion that socked him right in the belly. Had a woman ever before looked at him with such desire? Did she know what a terrific turn-on it was just to be looked at like that? He felt a sudden need to strip her clothes off her and run his hands slowly over her exquisite body inch by slow inch. Instead, he stepped forward and took the wine bottle from her hands.

"Here, let me," he said, stepping back again. "Corkscrew?"

She handed it over, and he noticed her eyes were suddenly skittish. He focused on the wine. Holding the bottle at a slight angle, he twisted the screw into the cork and eased it out. He pushed the bottle down into the ice bucket and wrapped it with a folded towel.

"Can I help with anything in the kitchen?" she asked, her voice unusually husky, but he shook his head.

"Nope. Everything's ready. When the Scrivners get here, I'll just wheel it in and we'll eat."

She nodded, hands folded demurely at her waist. "The, um, turkey looks great," she said. "I can't wait to taste it."

"I hope you like it," he told her, "because we're going to be eating this bird for a while. Four people aren't going to do it justice."

"I'm sure I won't mind at all," she returned. "I'll bet you make a dynamite turkey sandwich."

"A dynamite turkey salad sandwich," he corrected, and then for some reason they both laughed.

The Scrivners came in, and they all stood around for a moment while Walker and Imogene exclaimed over the turkey and the table. Then Bonnie lit the candles, and the men helped the ladies into their chairs, after which Walker asked for the privilege of pouring the wine while Owen went to fetch the serving carts. He pushed in the desserts first, then, while everyone drooled over the pumpkin pie and the cherry mousse and the plates of fruit-filled meringue tarts, he went back for the side dishes. Besides the rich dressing, peas, sweet potato casserole, cranberry salad, and yeast rolls, he'd prepared steamed asparagus with hollandaise and acorn squash baked with lemon and cinnamon, as well as a fragrant gravy teeming with sliced boiled egg and leeks.

It was a memorable meal. Owen received their compliments with pride, ate heartily, and shared techniques with Imogene. They took their time, savoring each dish and making conversation. The Scrivners mentioned their son occasionally, commenting that he would appreciate this dish or that and then saying laughingly how he'd have preferred a good burger and fries anytime.

"Just like a teenager," Imogene said, her eyes misting.

His own impulse was to let the topic drop right there and trot out another, then he heard Bonnie saying, "Tell us about him," and suddenly Walker and Imogene both were rattling on and on about a boy who seemed wonderfully typical in every way, from the shoes he wore to the pranks he pulled and his grades in school. It seemed, somehow, as if it helped them to talk, though Owen had assumed the opposite, and in an odd way it helped him to hear, to know that such a loss could be overcome though not "gotten over." He began to understand that some things never went away but could be endured and countered with other joys so that life continued to be worth living. His own losses and problems seemed insignificant by comparison, and he was deeply grateful that Bonnie had been here to draw out the Scrivners and make him a party to the experience.

They were all friends by the time dessert was served, as comfortable with one another as friends could be. Pleasantly stuffed and relaxed to the point of enervation, they left the table to wander into the parlor, where he happily laid a fire and lit it. After a while, he knew that if he didn't get up and clear the table right away, it would still be there in the morning. He made himself do it, glad when Bonnie insisted on helping out.

"We've enjoyed everything tremendously," Imogene said. "Too tremendously, I'm afraid. I think I could sleep for a week."

"You go right on up when you're ready," Bonnie told them, "and let us know if we can do anything else."

"My dear," Walker said warmly, "you've simply given us the most enjoyable day we've had in many months. Our thanks."

Owen thought to himself that it had been worth every degree of his effort to make such a thing possible, but he knew that he hadn't done it alone, and he was about to say so to Bonnie when, as they crossed the foyer to the dining room, the telephone rang.

"Want me to get it?" he asked, and she nodded.

"I'll start clearing."

He grabbed up the turkey platter and carried that into the kitchen, setting it upon the counter and reaching for the

phone in the same smooth movement. The voice that replied to his greeting possessed a decidedly Texas drawl.

"Mr. Ketter, I presume."

Owen raised a brow. "Yes?"

"Thomas Maxwell, Bonnie's brother. Is she around?"

"Sure. She's clearing the dining room. I'll give her a
shout."

"To tell you the truth," the voice replied, "it'd be better
if she called back. Mom's feeling kind of low, you know,
this being the very first time one of her babies has missed
the big day. She doesn't know I've called, see, and I'd like
her not to."

The big day? Owen cocked his head to one side, wondering if he was getting this right. "I thought your family
didn't celebrate Thanksgiving," he said.

Thomas laughed. "Where'd you get a crazy idea like
that? Thanksgiving is *the* big day of the year here."

The big day. Now why had Bonnie told him otherwise?
He was certain he hadn't gotten it wrong. He drew his
brows together in perusal. "Let me ask you something,
Thomas," he said, "does your family have a cook?"

"Sort of," came the careful reply. "That is, we have a
cook, but Mom doesn't let her do much. Dad's always
teasing her about paying the cook to stand around and
wring her hands, but that's Mom. She's a real hands-on
sort, won't even have poor Gladys in the house on holidays."

The cook's day off! As if the family didn't pull out all the
stops and partake of a special dinner. But why let him think
otherwise? *So you wouldn't feel guilty about having her
here, moron*, said a small voice inside his head. Owen
nearly hung up the phone then and there to go and shake
her and tell her what a sweetheart she was, but at the last

instant realized what he was doing and jerked the phone back to his ear.

"I—I'll have her call. And thanks. I mean, goodbye."

He hung up and ran a hand over the back of his neck. He hadn't suspected a thing, nitwit that he was, and probably he'd never have known if he hadn't answered the phone call. What did a man do with a woman so determined to be considerate and helpful and . . .

Bonnie herself cut off the train of his thought by merely appearing. She was pushing one cart and pulling another heaped with dirty dishes, and she smiled even as she looked up. He wanted to take her in his arms right then, but didn't dare.

"Who was it?" she asked, coming around the end of the counter to get a dishcloth. Owen wasn't sure how to answer, so he just stood there while she wrapped the cloth around her slender waist and presented him her back so that he could tie it. "One of your brothers?" she prodded gently, looking at him over her shoulder. The pose gave her light eyes an exotic slant that was highly distracting. His hands fumbled with the ends of the dishcloth. She turned back to face him, concern turning her pretty mouth down at the corners. "Owen?" she said softly, her hand coming up to finger the lapel of his jacket.

He felt weak all at once and leaned back against the edge of the counter, his heart pounding. "You didn't want me to be alone here with the Scrivners, did you?" he asked softly.

She laughed, the sound husky and warm. "What are you talking about?"

"Your brother Thomas wants you to call your mother," he told her. "She's sad because you missed the big day."

Bonnie bit her lip. "Oops."

"You stayed for me," he said, and she just looked at him, her reply in her eyes. He felt strong suddenly, invincible. He straightened and settled his hands at her waist, and as he'd known she would, she stepped forward, bringing her slender body against his, her hands sliding up and around his neck. He bent his head and touched his lips to hers, remembering the look of desire in her eyes and the sound of her laughter and the graceful beauty of her hands as she lifted her wineglass. She melted against him, opening her mouth to his, yielding, giving. He wrapped his arms around her and deepened the kiss, saying to himself that this was what a man did with a woman like Bonnie Maxwell, this and more. He broke the kiss and took her hand, nuzzling her delicate ear.

"Come with me," he whispered, and in his mind he was already moving toward the bedroom, stripping the clothes from his body, holding her in the crook of his arm as he gently levered his weight atop her. It was what they both wanted, had wanted for some time. He stepped away from the counter toward the center of the room. She did not move with him. Her hand stayed in his, but she did not go with him. He looked back at her. Her eyes were wide and frank and soft, her head lifted at the end of her long, smooth neck.

"I'll go with you, Owen," she said, "and gladly. But you've got to know that you're the one who stepped over the line."

Him? He was stepping over the line? He, who'd sworn off women, who'd pieced his life together shard by delicate shard after the last one? Tish had been nice and sweet and giving in the beginning, too, then she'd cut his heart out and handed it to him in a sandwich bag, and here he was crossing that same line again, falling in love, offering up his heart to the butcher so she could make ground meat out of it. What was wrong with him, anyway? Was he so damned pathetic that he *had* to get carved up? He dropped her hand as though it already held the knife, and the hurt look on her face made him want to kick himself and start throwing things. He didn't want to hurt her. He just didn't want to *be* hurt.

"I must be out of my mind," he said, and saw her wince. He quickly stepped toward her, his hands coming up to pull her to him, but he knew comforting her would be a mistake and pushed them down again. "Damn it!" He was angrier at himself than at her, but she didn't know that, and it occurred to him that it might be just as well. He turned away, gritting his teeth and clenching his fists.

"All right," she said quietly, "just remember that this was your idea, too. I want you to know, Owen, that whatever happens between us is up to you, and it always will be—no matter how much I want it."

He heard the patter of her footsteps as she hurried from the room, each one a blow to him, and wondered which of them was the real fool or if there was any way to keep them both from being hurt.

Chapter Seven

During the weeks that followed, Bonnie never said another word about that kiss. In fact, except for Owen's own sense of guilt and confusion, it might never have happened. She kept herself busy redecorating the bedrooms in the house, and he let her because she had been such a good sport about everything else, but he couldn't help grousing a little about all the money she was spending, money he didn't have and his pride wouldn't let him accept unconditionally. She just laughed, of course, and pointed out once again that bedspreads and curtains and rugs and lamps and framed pictures were all things she could take with her if she left.

If. She always said if she left. After everything, it was still if.

They had guests arriving and departing all the time, but the house was never full or even close to it. Still, she insisted on laying in a supply of new towels, all spotlessly white because that was easiest to clean, and she, as she pointed out, had to clean them. The rooms, however, were done over in living color, soft tones of teal, mauve, lavender, and melon, according to Bonnie—green, pink, purple, and orange to him. He favored the green and orange, which didn't seem to surprise her a bit, but he wasn't about to let her redecorate his room, too. She accepted the veto good-naturedly and went on about her business.

The second week of December, she began to decorate for Christmas. Owen had never seen the like of evergreen boughs and crystal lights and multicolored glass ornaments. There were angels with gossamer wings and brass trumpets and pinecones and tiny pottery villages and an endless variety of painted wooden trinkets that were undoubtedly Victorian. She put a crèche in the front yard, complete with baby Jesus, hovering angels, animals, and megawatt stars, which had the neighbors standing around staring in admiration, and she brought in a tree that four men had to carry and around which the whole parlor had to be rearranged.

Owen grumbled and pointed out that they didn't need ninety-nine per cent of the "junk" she was "throwing around the house," but Bonnie just laughed and called him "Scrooge" and told him not to worry because the Christmas Spirit was on its way. He thought she was just being cute until his youngest brother arrived on the twenty-second. He was in the kitchen, naturally, stirring bourbon soaked cherries and raisins into the walnut cake he would serve with mulled wine on Christmas Eve, when a particularly elfin giggle made him look up and right into the brown eyes of one of the most precious faces in the world.

"Amy!" He dropped the spoon just in time to catch her as she flew at him, all knees and elbows and ponytails in a five-year-old package as sweet as candy. "Where did you come from?"

"Denver," was the giggled answer.

"Where are your mom and dad?"

"Front and center, old man." He looked to the doorway where Paul and his wife, Rachel, stood arm-in-arm with Bonnie. "Good to see you, Owen," Paul said, and suddenly it was Christmas, after all.

Nathan and his wife, Donna, showed up the next day with seven-year-old Phoebe, Pheebs to her Uncle O, and all anyone could talk about was what a bang-up job Bonnie had done with the house. Owen had to admit that the place had never looked better, and he couldn't help being grateful to Bonnie for all that she'd done, especially getting Paul and Nathan there with their families. He tried to tell her that evening, when everyone came in from a sleigh ride she had arranged, how very much it meant to him, but he just wound up tongue-tied and frustrated and red in the face. She patted his shoulder and smiled and whispered, "Merry Christmas, partner," so maybe he didn't do such a bad job, after all. But it required something more, much more, and that was why he went out and bought the snowboard.

It was the only thing he could think of, and he didn't have the slightest doubt that she would put it to good use, but he was still nervous about it, hoping she would like it and that it would say everything he wanted to but couldn't put into words. He had it professionally wrapped, not trusting himself to do even a passable job, and hid it in the shed out back where she wasn't likely to be poking around.

Everyone was having a great time. Bonnie had organized everything, right down to a scenic tour of the lights and historic homes, and to Owen's surprise his family was saying it was their best trip to Leadville ever. They even went along with the caroling she'd planned for Christmas Eve, everyone but him, not that they needed his "bull moose bass," as Nathan jokingly put it. While they were away, he told himself that he could have gone along and kept his mouth shut. No one would have cared. But then he decided to put his time to good use. He built a fire in the parlor and popped a tub of popcorn and heated up some apple cider with spiced apple rings, cinnamon sticks, and butter for the returning carolers. It turned out to be a pretty good idea, because they were all shivering when they got back, and the girls loved the popcorn and cider. They started stringing some for the tree but wound up wearing it around their necks, instead, little girl Christmas jewelry.

When Bonnie called him out into the foyer and presented him with the Santa suit, he thought she was nuts at first. But then Amy and Pheebs started giggling and singing corny versions of the carols, and he remembered that Christmas without children was just another day and agreed to play Santa on Christmas morning. They made another plan, whereby he could pull off the Santa impersonation, and clued in his brothers and their wives. With the help of their parents, Amy and Pheebs were to awaken early and go downstairs on their own, where they would catch "Santa" in the act of delivering their toys. The adults would watch from the front porch, sneaking down in their coats with cameras after the kids had left the room. Santa would wish the youngsters a merry Christmas and beat a hasty retreat, after which old Uncle O would come in and "call down" the others.

It went like clockwork. Pheebs was the first one into the parlor on Christmas morning, and "Santa" was properly surprised. She bought it lock, stock, and barrel and even helped him get out the goodies before Amy arrived, sleepy-eyed and a little grumpy.

"A-my!" Phoebe scolded. "Don't you see who this is?" At which point Amy opened her mouth and shrieked in utter delight.

Owen spun some yarn about Leadville being so high up that it was always his last stop and asked if he didn't usually deliver for them in Denver. He congratulated Phoebe on her good grades in school and told her she better lay off that little boy in her class, which brought gasps and fervent promises. For Amy, he commented on how hard she'd worked to learn to write all the ABCs and suggested that she show a little more enthusiasm when her mother asked her to visit old Mrs. Monroe down the street, even though her house did smell like medicine. After that he invited them to see what he'd brought, and while they were tearing into the packages, he made his escape, slipping out just before Uncle O came in barefoot and wearing jeans and a T-shirt with his hair all mussed up. They were breathless with excitement, thoroughly convinced that they'd caught Santa in the act of delivering toys, and Owen admitted to the other adults later that he'd never had such fun.

"You need a couple kids of your own," Paul told him with a grin, but Owen knew his chance at that had already passed him by.

"Forty-six is a little late to start a family," he pointed out gruffly, but Bonnie had to put in her two cents worth.

"My dad was fifty when my baby brother, Ron, was born," she said. "My *Mom* was forty-six."

"Gotcha!" Nathan said with a wiggle of his eyebrows. Like Owen, he already had a head full of gray hair, but his brows were a dark, dusty blond. Owen glowered at him, but he couldn't help thinking that Nathan was only a couple of years younger than he was. Maybe it wasn't too late. And maybe he was getting prematurely senile, too, which would explain why he was thinking like this.

Owen knew that Nathan thought he and Bonnie were more than business partners and friends. They all did. And maybe they were right. Maybe somehow, without his no-

ticing, they'd become a couple. He didn't know what to
think anymore. Bonnie seemed to fit into his life so easily,
as though she belonged there, and yet he couldn't forget
that she was leaving, for undoubtedly she would, if only
because he couldn't find the words to help her stay.

Still, sometimes it seemed as if she could read him like a
book. How could she know, otherwise, just the right thing
to get him? When he opened the box with her name on the
tag as giver and saw the heavy pewter frame with those two
darling faces, Amy's and Pheeb's, smiling up at him, he
knew nothing could have pleased him more. It was perfect, not too fussy but not plain, and the pictures were
wonderful, without that posed look that made everyone
seem pained. Tendrils of Amy's dark hair had slipped free
of her ponytail and wafted softly about her face, the brown
eyes that belonged to her mother sparkling with mischief,
while Pheeb's were a startling blue, her ash blond locks
curling about her ears with the same wild abandon evident
in her gap-toothed smile. He laughed aloud with the sheer
pleasure of looking at it and couldn't wait for her to open
the box he'd brought in from the toolshed. But he bided his
time, knowing she thought that big box way in the back
must belong to someone else, and enjoyed the clamor of his
family about him.

Finally all the gifts had been dispersed except that one.
Bonnie herself was helping get them out from under that
gargantuan tree, and he was watching when she pulled that
big, ungainly box toward her, read the name on the tag, and
lifted a hand to her heart in surprise. She glanced up, and
her gaze collided with his and held a moment before moving back to the box. She was on her knees beside the tree,
wearing ruby red sweats and a matching ribbon in her hair.
Her face bore not a speck of makeup of any kind, and on
her stocking feet were those fluffy houseshoe things that

made her look as if she wore powder puffs on her toes. She looked like a big kid, especially when she started ripping away the shiny gold paper and wide red ribbon. He watched her strip the brown cardboard box of its dressing, then shake the top off and paw through the crumpled tissue paper. She paused when her hand found the smooth rounded edge, then slowly lifted one end of the bright yellow board free, her mouth forming a wide O, and Owen smiled, seeing her delight.

Paul caught sight of the board then, and promptly put aside the set of socket wrenches Owen had bought him to have a closer look. Bonnie offered it up with glee for his inspection, and by that time everyone had been alerted and was gathering around. Bonnie laughed delightedly as the men made envious sounds over the snowboard. It was the newest model with the aft "dip and lip" that allowed the boarder to put a foot back, out of strap, in order to perform stunts. The other women thought it looked dangerous, but the men were intrigued, and when Bonnie got up and slipped away from them to come and thank him, he knew he couldn't have chosen better. She was thrilled. She popped down on the arm of his chair, her arm sliding naturally across his shoulders.

"You spent too much," she said. Then, "I love it!"

He felt horribly conspicuous even though no one else was looking at them, and squirmed a little. "I'm glad." It came out all rumbly and thick. "You, ah, you've done so much work on, um, *my* lodge and... Well, you deserve it." He wondered if she'd bought that. Something told him she didn't, and when he glanced up, he saw that her eyes were swimming with unshed tears. He looked away quickly, but not before those eyes pierced him to the heart. Wordlessly, he found himself groping for her hand, then squeezing it, then brusquely putting it aside and getting up. "Breakfast time," he muttered, striding away, but when he looked back, she was still sitting there, watching him, her eyes full of an emotion he dared not contemplate, and for the first time it occurred to him that this time Bonnie had never said a word about going home to Texas for the holiday. And neither had he.

Maybe they were more than friends, more than business partners. Maybe a fellow could have more than one chance—if he could just bring himself to try.

Bonnie had never been so happy. The place was near to full on this next to the last day of the Christmas vacation season. The Intellectual Fun Club of Houston had seen to that, and they weren't all Larry Carpenters, thank goodness. Christmas itself had been wonderful. Owen had been thrilled to have his family there, and the girls had made everything such fun. She couldn't get over Owen playing Santa Claus and told herself for the umpteenth time what a good father he'd make. She'd hated to see the girls and their parents go, but she was glad for the new easiness that had developed between Owen and herself since their departure. Were it not for the slick brochure she held in her hand and the note attached, her world would be delightfully carefree.

She put the brochure and the note from Harv back into her bureau drawer, determined not to think about it until later. This was the last official celebration of the holiday season, and the last night of the old year. Tomorrow would begin a new year and a whole new phase in her partnership with Owen. She just knew it. She could feel it. Every time he looked at her lately, every time he smiled, she could feel the emotion building, growing, swelling between them, straining to break free. Perhaps tonight. Surely he wouldn't deny her a dance. He'd sounded enthusiastic when she'd proposed that option for their New Year's Eve party.

Thoughts of the party preparations intruded. Had she asked Anne and Martin Ferguson to bring all those CDs Owen had told her about? Had Celia Zimmer responded to her invitation? Did anyone think to count the little champagne bottles? Should they tell everyone about the mock champagne punch or just let them think they were getting intoxicated? They should move some chairs from the dining room to the parlor, but that easy chair and the rockers had to go into Owen's room temporarily. They just took up too much room. Oh, and the rug. The rug had to be rolled up. She'd get some of the Intellectual Fun Clubbers to help. After all, it was their party, too.

Working quickly, she put the finishing touches on her makeup, then stepped back from the mirror to get a good look. The frogs on the front of her red Chinese tunic were hooked up crooked. She corrected them, her red-painted nails flashing as she twisted the covered buttons out of and into loops. That done, she straightened again. A green and black embroidered dragon swooped over her shoulder and flew down her front, talons uncurled, tail lashing out behind. The slinky black pants she wore beneath the slashed tunic were slim and long, draping comfortably over the ankle straps of her high heels.

She had parted her hair in the center and brushed it back behind her shoulders, her bangs left to fall smoothly forward. Red enamel beads clipped to her earlobes gave a nice effect, but she decided the gold bracelets were too much and took them off, preferring the clean, slender lines of her bare arms. Bonnie had decided long ago that her height and vivid coloring called for a kind of stark elegance, and that one fashion rule had served her well. It served now. The dragon was more than enough embellishment, even for

New Year's Eve. She went out to see to the last-minute details, feeling sexy and graceful in her high heels.

She'd hardly gotten the rug stowed away when the first outside guests showed up, early. Everyone was in a party mood, it seemed, despite the snow-covered roads and ditches. The plows had already been out, but the snow just kept coming down in a steady fall, covering what they'd cleared with white, glistening powder, inches and inches of it. The weather service was predicting more than a foot by dawn, but from the way it was coming down, Bonnie would say their estimate was on the low end of possibilities. Jack Hampton and his date agreed, though the prospects didn't seem to dampen their spirits any, and the same went for the Fergusons when they arrived, bearing a suitcase full of CDs.

Owen, wearing navy trousers and a big soft gray sweater with the sleeves pushed up, had set up a table full of what he called appetizers in the dining room, though it looked more like a full-blown buffet to Bonnie, and another of drinks, including the punch. When the lights went down and the music was cranked up, laughter and talk percolated, and a couple moved onto the dance floor in the parlor without the slightest prodding from the hostess.

In no time at all, the house was overflowing with laughing, chatting, munching, sipping, dancing people. Bonnie started a dice game, with painted matchsticks substituting for money, in the back of the foyer, and set up a pair of easels for a round of Fast Draw in a corner of the dining room. Downstairs, the pool table and television were both surrounded by players and supporters. The sounds of balls cracking against one another and lasers zapping incoming aliens were all but drowned out by the cheering, so naturally someone cranked up the stereo another notch, and the whole house rocked and rolled toward midnight.

Finally, after hours of this revelry, things toned down a bit. Someone switched off most of the lights upstairs, and the music took on a slow, easy, dreamy quality. Bonnie found herself leaning in the doorway between foyer and dining room, gently swaying to the music and wishing Owen would ask her to dance. Then he appeared at her elbow, his big hands spanning her waist as he physically moved her forward into the vacant entryway. There, at the foot of the broad staircase, he took her into his arms and held her close as they danced to the music of a lilting piano backed by a plaintive, bluesy saxophone. Too soon, the music ended, but still Owen held her. She laid her head upon his shoulder, her fingers intertwined with his, and sighed with joy, her lips finding the sensitive curve of his neck. Then someone called out, "Two minutes to midnight!"

"Champagne time," Owen said softly, and they pulled apart to walk hand in hand into the dining room and break a seal on a cardboard box of plastic glasses. He had filled a large barrel with crushed ice and the small bottles of champagne, and while Bonnie turned on the dining room lights, he positioned it for easy access. Their guests poured into the room, mobbing the replenished food table, glass cartons, and wine barrel. The music cranked up again. Games, pool tables, and dance floor were temporarily abandoned as everyone prepared for the big moment.

In the middle of the happy chaos, Owen's eyes met hers, and in that instant she knew they were thinking the same thing. Quickly, before anyone could notice, she snatched two glasses. Owen grabbed her hand, two bottles in the crook of his arm, and they literally ran through the kitchen into the mudroom. Owen snagged a coat as they ran for the door, tossing it over her head and shoulders.

They burst out into the backyard, laughing for no apparent reason, except that the snow was falling and the air was crisp to the point of breaking and the people they'd left behind were happy because of them. Bonnie gasped as her feet sank into cold snow. With hardly a break in stride, Owen swept her up into his arms and carried her to the gazebo. Snow had piled up on the ledges and seats, but the floor was clear in the center, and there he put her down to stand on her own feet. He put his arms around her and drew her close, but she could feel him shivering and pulled back to shrug off the coat. She helped him put it on, holding it as he slid his arms into the sleeves, then pulling it up over his shoulders before slipping inside with him, her arms about his solid waist. He pulled the front of the coat together over her back and wrapped his arms about her. She had never felt so warm and safe. Together they watched the snow fall.

When the cheer went up inside the house, marking the hour, he placed his hands over her ears and tilted her head back. She went up on tiptoe and lifted her chin. His mouth came down and melded with hers, gently at first and then with growing pressure as his arms slid around her once more. She parted her teeth, and his tongue entered her mouth, tasting its silky walls and roof and parrying with her own as it curled in welcome. His hands roamed over her back in tandem, then parted company, one splaying between her shoulder blades, the other across her hips, pressing her to him. She slipped her fingers beneath the hem of his sweater to feel the taut skin and solid muscle banking the gentle valley of his spine just before it disappeared below the waistband of his slacks.

She was weak with the joy of his nearness and hot inside with desire, yet strangely content to stand there with her mouth joined to his. The breath from their nostrils fogged the air within the gazebo, and the falling snow curtained them without, so that they were cocooned together in privacy, and a cozy cocoon it was. After a long while he broke the kiss and just held her while the snow fell and the music played on, muffled by distance and walls and the laughter of friends. She wanted to say that she loved him, that she would stay with him always and never tire of his touch or kiss or grow impatient with his moods or hold herself back from fulfilling his needs. She wanted to hear him say it, to know they would never part, to give herself away and get him in return. But she knew that this was not the time. They had hills to climb yet, hurdles to leap, and barriers to pull down. It was enough now to have started in the right direction, to have embarked upon the path.

"Cold?" he asked, hugging her to him inside the coat.

She shook her head. "Just a little tired."

He walked her to the bench, swept it clean with his hand, and sat down, pulling her onto his lap.

"It's wet," he said, as if he needed an explanation.

"Good," she whispered, snuggling close.

He chuckled and stroked her hair. "You're very beautiful. Did you know that?"

She smiled. "I don't care whether I am or not, as long as you think so."

"Well, I do," he told her, "but I have to admit that I wish I didn't."

"Why?"

He cupped her face with his big hand, and his eyes held hers. "I want to make love to you," he said.

It was time to be honest. "I know," she told him quietly.

"But I won't."

"I know that, too."

He smiled and kissed her forehead. "Beautiful and smart," he said. Then, with a sigh, "I wish it could be different."

"It can," she promised him, "if you'll let it."

He shook his head doubtfully. "I don't know. I've thought so much about it. You don't know how hard it is, Bonnie. No matter what they tell you, love hurts."

"Not always," she said. "Sometimes..." She brushed his cheek with her fingertips. "Sometimes it can be so wonderful, when the people and the time are right."

"Maybe," he whispered, but his gaze was on her mouth, and she knew instinctively that she had but to turn her head a certain way to welcome his kiss.

She did it without even thinking and felt herself borne down and backward in the cradle of his arm, his mouth plying hers hungrily. She ran her hands over his chest, feeling the knobby softness of his sweater and the hard muscles underneath, then at his gentle urging moved her arm aside to allow him the fullness of her breast against his palm. His tongue thrust deeply into her mouth, his head bobbing as he worked that kiss. She let him take it as far as he dared, welcoming every touch, knowing they were limited to this and nothing more, loving him with silence and acquiescence, without demand or expectation.

After a long while she felt him pulling back. He lifted his mouth from hers but kept close, his nose nuzzling her cheek. Slowly he tamped down the flames of desire, getting himself together, taking himself in hand. It was over now, and they both knew it. They had gone as far together as they could go—this time—but still they lingered, holding on to each other and watching the snow fall in big lacy flakes against the black of the night.

They heard their names called and ignored it, saw the headlights of the faint of heart as they pulled out early and went home, tires crunching over the new snow. A breeze built drifts against the house and Owen's truck and the toolshed and the trunks of the trees. The whole world grew white from the ground up, and the din of the party seemed to fill it with sound. At last, they knew they could delay no longer, and, with a final look, parted.

Bonnie got to her feet, suddenly cold. Owen slipped out of the coat and wrapped it around her, folding the collar up about her chin. He led her to the edge of the gazebo and stepped down into the snow, looking up at her, her hand in his. She brushed his hair back from his forehead, thinking, *silver and gold, gold and silver*. The real things were nothing compared to this man.

"Happy New Year," he whispered.

She smiled and answered, "Happy New Year, Owen." He let go of her hand, and she stepped off into nothing, his arms lifting her against him. He carried her to the house, moving slowly and reluctantly despite the penetrating cold. The step to the back door was covered afresh, so he didn't put her down until they were inside, maneuvering with elbows and shoulders to get through the door. She brushed the snowflakes from his head and shoulders as he replaced the coat on its peg. They started inside to resume their roles as host and hostess, but then she thought of what she must look like, having necked in the gazebo on a cold winter night.

"Wait," she said. "I'd better powder my nose."

He pointed her toward the hallway that led to his room. "Go through that way and slip upstairs. I'll make some noise in the kitchen. There are still some cheese puffs drying out in the oven, anyway."

She thanked him with a smile and moved away on tiptoe. It was cold in that back hallway, so she hurried, taking care not to make noise. Quietly she opened the door to his room. The light was on, and there were coats piled on his bed. She didn't stop but moved swiftly across the room from door to bedpost to door. There she paused before slipping out into the back of the foyer to throw a longing glance over her shoulder.

Would Owen ever welcome her to his heart and his bed? She knew she wouldn't have one without the other, for Owen was not that kind of man. His feelings ran deep and wide, never shallow or false. It was all or nothing with him, nothing or everything he had to give. Tonight had been the exception, and she was thankful, for it helped to know that she could move him even a little toward loving again, but she was a long way from knowing that kind of all-consuming emotion of which he was capable. She wanted it. Oh, how she wanted it.

Patience, she counseled herself. Patience and time, that was what she needed, real time, not just the three or four months left her. Profit would buy her time, and advertising would bring her profit if she could get it out soon enough to fill this house during Spring Break. She had to try again to get Owen to agree. She had to. It was her only hope and her greatest fear.

I'll do it, she promised herself, *somehow, I will.*

She heard a door slam in the kitchen, and a pan rattle as it hit the floor. Someone said, "That's where he is. Should've known." Someone else spoke, too, but footsteps carried the words away. Bonnie slipped out into the foyer, around the end of the staircase, and up the stairs. In her room, she powdered her face and applied lipstick and brushed her hair. Then she took the brochure from the bureau door and pinned it to the wall where she'd be sure to see it.

Soon, she pledged, *soon.* Confidence buoyed, she went down again to their guests and the new year.

Chapter Eight

They struggled through the first day of the new year at a snail's pace, cleaning up, putting back, throwing away, but by nightfall the house was back to normal. They didn't talk about the night before. What was there to say? Bonnie wanted Owen, loved him. Owen wanted Bonnie but was uncertain, even afraid. He seemed to think he would always be so. She hoped that he would change with time. Neither could tell what would be.

What occupied Bonnie's mind was how she could get Owen to accept that brochure tacked to the wall in her room. It didn't help that when Harvey Pendergast called ostensibly to wish them each a happy new year, what he actually said to her was, "Get that brochure out. Get it out *now* or finish the season in red ink—again. And, Bonnie, Owen was right about his ex-brother-in-law. Archie Belton wants his head on a spike, so for God's sake, don't miss that next payment. Don't even make it late."

It was not the sort of message to give her unfettered hope for the new year, but neither was she ready to pack up a moving van and go home to Texas. Harvey was right, after all. That brochure, or a few hundred like it, could be the difference between profit and loss. She couldn't blame him if there was more at stake than the business.

Damned if you do, and damned if you don't, she thought. Bringing up the idea of advertising might make Owen mad enough to throw her out, but not bringing it up was certain failure. She'd simply have to dig in and not back down this time, no matter how mad he got. If he threatened to throw her out, she'd just refuse to go. They had a deal, and she'd make him stick to it, whatever the cost. Otherwise they were both going to lose.

She had no choice, really, but it made sense to pick her moment. The moment did not come that first long day of the new year, or the next, for they spent that day seeing off their guests and cleaning up after them. Owen helped. Bonnie stripped and remade the beds and laundered the dirty linens, while he vacuumed and swept and dusted. They divided the bathrooms, scrubbing, sweeping, disinfecting until each one was spotless. By evening, the lodge was empty except for the two of them, and clean enough for inspection. They had a small party coming in the next day, and another on the fifth, followed by a group of six adults and four preschoolers on the eighth of January. Bonnie decided it was now or never.

She waited until dinner was over and they'd cleaned up the kitchen. Then she poured them each a glass of fruity red wine and suggested they drink it in the parlor. There, before a lovely fire that danced to the soft sound of background music, she pulled the folded brochure from the pocket of her jeans and handed it to him. The exterior pictures had been taken with a zoom lens from a distance of more than a block. There were also some shots of the town, but only a partial floor plan of the interior. The descriptions were apt. Prices were reported correctly. Owen's cooking was touted, and a paragraph had been inserted detailing the recreational possibilities other than skiing. On the back beside the address was a map showing Leadville in relation to Denver, Aspen, and Vail.

He gave it a thorough going-over, the only indication of his pending reaction a dangerously flexing muscle in his jaw. Bonnie made herself wait and concentrated on holding her wineglass steady, despite her quaking insides. When he'd done with it, Owen got up and walked to the fireplace, then flicked the brochure inside and turned away, drinking deeply from his glass. Bonnie closed her eyes, knowing what she had to do.

"That doesn't mean anything," she said evenly. "There are others."

"Oh? You're telling me you've already spent God only knows how much on this harebrained scheme and for that reason I ought to let you spend more?" His tone was caustic in the extreme.

"It isn't a harebrained scheme," she defended reasonably.

"The hell it isn't!" he came back. "You knew I wouldn't go for it, and that makes it a harebrained scheme!"

"I knew you wouldn't like it," she said, "but you're intelligent enough to think logically, and logic demands—"

"Demands nothing!" he yelled. "No one demands of Owen Ketter! I promised myself long ago that no one would ever again be in a position to demand anything of me!"

Bonnie put aside her drink and came to her feet. "Owen, please. You're twisting my words. I'm not demanding anything. I'm just trying to make you understand that this is necessary."

"You know how I feel about it!" he told her roughly.

"Yes," she admitted. "But, darling, that doesn't change the facts. Everything depends on Spring Break. We have to show a profit this season. That means we must advertise. The most expensive part is already out of the way, why can't we—"

"We!" he exploded. "We aren't doing this. *You* are."

"To help *us!*"

"There is no *us!*" he insisted, turning his back.

For a moment Bonnie couldn't speak, and when she did, it wasn't any more well considered than what she'd already said. "There could be," she said softly. "Wasn't that what last night was about?"

He set his wineglass on the mantel, gripped its edge, and stared into the fire. Finally he answered. "No."

She closed her eyes, lips curling under, teeth clamping down. It wasn't true. He wouldn't admit it, but he could love her. She knew it, and suddenly nothing was more important than making him know it, too. She went to him, gripped his shoulder and arm, willed him to listen.

"Owen, if there was nothing between us, last night would not have happened. You aren't the sort of man who casually makes love to a woman. I know you wouldn't have touched me if it hadn't meant something to you. You're much too fair for that."

He shrugged her away. "What about you?" he wanted to know. "Is this what you call playing fair? Using physical attraction to get your way! Bartering your body! Is that what last night was really about?"

She had to clench her hand in the front of her sweatshirt to keep from slapping him. "I can't believe you said that!"

"I can't believe you had that damned thing printed knowing—"

"Yes, I know all about your stupid pride!" she screamed. "I know you don't want a partner! I know you've been hurt! But I also know you're going to lose this place if you don't let me help you!"

"I don't need your help!" he yelled back.

"You *need* this advertising campaign!"

They were right back where they'd started, which was miles apart, and they both knew it. Bonnie put her hands to her head, desperate for something to say that would reach him, but Owen had apparently heard enough already.

"To hell with it," he rumbled, and before she could so much as open her mouth again, he strode from the room.

She felt like throwing things, like kicking and screaming in rage until the frustration went away. Instead she plopped down in the easy chair, buried her face in her hands, and cried like a baby.

Owen huddled inside his coat and stamped his feet. He didn't know why he'd come here, except that he couldn't think of any other place to go. It had been the same way the night before. He'd brought her here because it was the only place he could think of where he could have her all to himself for a while, the only place outside of the bedroom, and he wouldn't do that. He had promised himself he wouldn't do that. He'd promised himself a lot of things, and so far he hadn't done such a hot job of making those promises come true.

When he'd first left Denver, he'd only wanted to get away from the pain. His job meant nothing to him anymore. Tish had stripped him of his home and his ambition and even many of his friends. But when he'd found this house, he'd known he'd found a place where he could build something again. Everything he had was invested in this place, every dollar, every emotion, every ounce of his energy.

He looked at the big, silent hulk that was his home, his business, and the focus of his life. It seemed empty and cold and forbidding, but he knew that it was warm and bright and welcoming inside. He'd hated the idea of sharing it, and he'd sworn that no one would ever be in a position to take it from him. Those were the reasons he hadn't wanted Bonnie. But he was sane enough to know that Bonnie was right. Without her, he was going to lose this place. It wasn't her fault he'd gotten behind in the payments. She wasn't to blame because people weren't beating a path to the door. In fact, she'd offered him the only real solution to the problem, though it meant getting in deeper with her than he'd ever intended. But maybe he'd already done that.

He turned around and looked at the bench where they'd sat together. It was covered with snow again and offered no hint that for a while he had been able to just put away the world and be with a woman again, that woman. Bonnie. She would never know how much he wanted to believe she was different, how badly he wanted to trust her. But he had believed before. He had trusted. It was too much to ask of him again. What angered him most was that he had no choice in the matter, not as far as the business was concerned. So it came down to what he was willing to sacrifice, his home and his business or his heart. Or did it?

They'd started as business partners. He didn't know when it had begun to be more than that; he only knew he couldn't let it be. All right, so what was a few extra thousand dollars? It only meant he'd have to work a little harder, stretch out the payoff a little longer. He'd have it back again, and Bonnie would lose nothing. If that damned brochure would do everything she claimed, business would pick up, and before long he could give her back every cent—with interest—every penny for the back payments, every nickel spent on materials, every dime's worth of pillows and rugs and towels. And then he'd be free again, on his own again. Nobody could touch him, and nobody could say he hadn't been fair.

He regretted those things he'd said. Deep down, he knew she was a decent, honest woman. He even believed that she cared for him. Now. What he didn't believe, couldn't believe, was that she'd never stop caring. So it had to stay business. *Keep it at that,* he told himself, *and you'll be all right. You'll both be all right if it stays business.* He knew what he had to do, but he couldn't stop himself from looking once more at that bench and remembering how for a while they had held the world at bay. But only for a while. It was always only for a while. That, too, he would remember.

He went into the house, hung the coat on a peg in the mudroom, and walked down the hall to his bedroom. He wanted to stay there. It had been a long day and he was tired, but sleep would have to wait. He went out the other door and walked through the foyer to the parlor. She wasn't there. He turned and looked up. A strip of light showed at the bottom of her door. He climbed the stairs and walked along the landing.

"Bonnie?" He rapped his knuckles lightly against the stained wood. "Bonnie, I need to talk to you."

"All right." Her voice was calm, unaccusing. "Come in."

He opened the door. She was sitting up in bed, the covers folded against her waist. Her hair lay sleekly against one shoulder. She wore an old football jersey that was all but threadbare, the number faded. "Where'd you get that?" he asked, glad to defer for a moment what he had come to say.

She looked down at herself. "This? About a century ago my dad played football. When I left home for college he gave it to me. I always think I'll put it away before it disintegrates, and then I always put it on and go to bed." She shrugged, as if to say she didn't know why she couldn't put it away. Owen remembered his own jersey folded away in a chest downstairs. Or was it in the attic? He put it out of mind.

"I came to apologize," he said, surprised by the ease of it.

She nodded. "I wish I could find a way to..." She let it trail off, seemingly uncertain what she'd intended.

He shook his head. "It's all right. You've done everything possible. I know I'm the problem, and, well, I'm not going to be, that's all. But I want you to know I'm going to pay you back. I swear I will."

"Pay me back for what?" she asked, a wrinkle appearing between her brows.

"The advertising."

She scrambled up to her knees. "You mean it? We're going to do it?"

"Yeah."

She sprang out of that bed, arms flying around his neck. The tail of her jersey hiked up to her seat, leaving those long legs bare. He looked down at that creamy length of leg and felt the thrust of her breasts against his chest, and his thoughts went instantly to her bed, the covers thrown back invitingly. She was babbling something in his ear, but it was just sound to him as he battled his masculine instinct. He closed his eyes and quite deliberately thought about Tish. Even then, extricating himself from those loving arms was one of the most difficult things he'd ever done. He felt a little better when she was standing in front of him, his hands holding her arms to her sides, but as he looked at that pretty face with its questioning expression, he couldn't help wondering if he was one of the great aberrations of nature or just its biggest fool. He had to take his hands off her before he could speak.

"Don't let's get carried away here," he said haltingly. "What I mean is, you're incredibly beautiful and I'm ... only human."

"So be human," she said, "or hasn't it occurred to you that I might actually want to be with you?"

He was shocked to hear her say that. It felt prudish and silly and dishonest, but he couldn't help it. "You shouldn't say things like that," he told her roughly. "You don't know what you're saying."

She lifted her chin, her eyes wide and soft and hopeful. "I know how I feel about you, and if you'd give yourself half a chance, you could feel the same way about me."

Now or never, he thought. *Say it now or don't say it at all.* He swallowed and pushed the words out fast. "You're wrong. This is business. It can't be anything else. It won't be."

She stood there for a long time, her chin aloft and stable, but then she dropped her gaze. "That's really how you want it?"

He felt free, saved. "Yes."   She nodded, and he imagined there were tears in her eyes, but when she looked up, those pale gray orbs were clear and frank. "All right, Owen," she said. "Just don't forget who made the rules."

Why, suddenly, did he feel deflated? He thought, obtusely, that she was certainly handling it well. *And what did you expect?* he asked himself. *Screams? Threats? Pleas?* He licked his lips, stiffened his spine. "It's for the best," he told her.

She turned her back, walked to the bed, got in, folded the covers beneath her arms. "Good night," she said, rolling onto her side and reaching for the lamp. The light flicked off.

He stared at her back, then closed the door and went away.

Bonnie managed to keep things relatively easy between them by simply behaving as if nothing had happened. It was not as if she chose to forget what she came to think of as "Owen's decision"; it was, instead, that she chose to pretend that he had never touched her, that she had never begun to think of him as the one man in the world to whom she wished to give her heart. The ploy worked well to a point—and that point happened to be the public perception of them as a couple. It came home to her on the evening of the very day the brochures went out in the mail, and it all began innocently when Anne and Martin Ferguson dropped by to invite them over for a movie and snacks.

"A reciprocal for New Year's Eve," Anne admitted, "but it won't be fancy. No one's willing to invite Owen to dinner. His cooking skills are much too intimidating."

She undoubtedly expected Owen to be amused and perhaps even flattered, but Bonnie could see that he was too uncomfortable being lumped together with her in their invitation to be anything else. Perhaps it was foolish of her, but she decided to extricate him from this delicate little situation. She put on a smile and lied with alarming ease.

"I'd love to," she said, "but I can't. I have a date."

She could not have calculated how strong an effect that little lie would have. Anne quite literally gasped, and Martin at once sent Owen a look of sheer pity. Owen himself scowled angrily. Bonnie was shocked. It had seemed the perfect solution. Not only did it spare Owen her company on the evening in question, but it rather confused the public idea of her and Owen being a couple. She'd assumed he'd be pleased. Instead, after the Fergusons had left them, he glowered as if she had publicly humiliated him.

"I'm sorry," she offered helplessly, uncertain even what she was sorry for.

"Don't be," he rumbled. "You're free to date whomever you please."

She opened her mouth to explain that she wasn't dating anyone, but he was already leaving the room. She felt persecuted, as if it were impossible to please him. First he was uneasy because his friends perceived them as a couple, then he was angry because she'd done something about it. She couldn't make much sense of it, unless... But it was folly to believe he was jealous. Wasn't it? Still, she couldn't quite put the notion out of mind. Perhaps that was why she accepted when Dr. Steven Clark asked her out less than forty-eight hours later.

It was a testament in a way to how quickly news could travel by word of mouth in a small town. They had dated before, of course, but he had backed off when everyone had assumed that she and Owen were a couple. Dr. Clark had gotten the news correcting that assumption from an overheard conversation. It seemed that on the particular evening in question he had stopped in for a drink at the same watering hole as the Fergusons and Kim Nabob. Of course, they were all acquainted, and he had apparently insinuated himself easily enough into the conversation. Everyone was wondering who Bonnie was dating. Steven didn't actually say so, but he didn't have to. Bonnie could tell from the carefully worded preface to his invitation that the main topic of conversation had been the identity of this mystery man. He didn't come right out and ask who he was, and she didn't volunteer any names. How could she since the man didn't even exist? Not that it seemed to make any difference to Steven. He seemed content so long as he

was not playing rival to Owen! Once he issued his own invitation—to dinner and a movie—and she had accepted, the
mystery man and any questions about him just seemed to
disappear. Bonnie was grateful for that much, for as it
turned out, Owen assumed that Steven Clark *was* the mystery man and that fit nicely with the lie she'd already told.
So it happened that on the night Owen visited the Fergusons, Bonnie actually *had* a date—with Dr. Steven Clark.
It was not the last.

Over the next month or so, Steven managed to see her a
couple of times a week. She was frankly surprised at how
much free time a small-town doctor could find, and she felt
a little guilty at moments because she seemed to be mo-
nopolizing all of his. Still, she grew increasingly thankful
for his attention, because as time passed it became obvious
that Owen Ketter was a better hand at suppressing his
emotion than she had assumed. Or perhaps she had misread all that had passed between them. It hardly mattered,
because Owen was clearly not jealous of Steven Clark. It
made Steven's careful courtship all the more special. It
helped her to continue believing that she was attractive despite Owen's rejection of her, and it provided a much
needed distraction. Otherwise she didn't know how she
would have gone on pretending that all was well.

Working with Owen was not the easy, natural activity it
had once been for her, but she was determined not to let it
show. She did not, after all, intend to punish him for de-
ciding to keep their relationship strictly business. That
would have been immature and foolish, especially as she
couldn't bear to think about having no relationship at all
with him. And so she put on a smile, made herself relax,
and tried to keep personal thoughts of Owen at bay whenever possible. The days were busy, and all the more so after those dearly won brochures began to produce results.

The phones seemed constantly to be ringing with inquiries from one travel agent or another, but that was poor comfort to Bonnie, except as it meant Owen would have no legitimate excuse for ending their business relationship. She supposed it was masochistic of her to want to hold on to the partnership, but she couldn't help it. Only Steven kept her from filling all her nights with even more pointless longing. For that reason alone she was fond of him, and she couldn't help thinking that it would be easier for everyone concerned if she could only love him.

Owen opened the door to the second delivery man with something akin to disbelief. Flowers, he could understand. It was Valentine's Day, after all. But his old buddy Steve seemed determined to go off the deep end where Bonnie was concerned, and as far as Owen could tell, Bonnie wasn't doing a thing to discourage him. In fact, she was doubtlessly encouraging him, not that she seemed to be losing her impressive equilibrium. One of the things Owen admired most about Bonnie was her even-temperedness, though no one knew better than he that she could be provoked.

He called her to the door and watched with hands on hips as she emerged from the rec room and walked toward him. She laughed when she saw the delivery man, then ran up for her purse and back down again while Owen made embarrassed, apologetic noises and tried not to glower. She tipped the delivery man, as she had the one before, with a crisp, folded bill, then took the enormous heart-shaped box into her arms. The dark red cellophane crackled merrily. Owen watched as she carried the box into the parlor, popped down in a chair, slipped off the wide pink ribbon, tore away the cellophane, and lifted the snow-white cardboard lid. The box must have contained four-dozen chocolates. She clapped her hands, selected one, bit into it, and rolled her eyes heavenward.

"I'm going to get fat!" She immediately amended that, as required by her generous nature. "We. We're going to get fat." She shoved the box at him. "Help yourself."

He shook his head from the doorway. He had no intention of eating Steve Clark's candy. "The good doctor isn't much on nutrition, is he?" He knew he sounded petty, and he hated that he did, but it was awfully difficult to watch a perfectly fine man make such a disgusting fool of himself.

She shrugged and selected another sweet. "Valentine's Day only comes once a year." Munching happily, she looked over the selection. "Ooh, here's a rum bonbon. You love rum bonbons. Pheebs told me."

"I love them, but I don't eat them," he grumbled. "Besides, Steve Clark didn't send candy—or flowers—to me."

She laughed. "Don't be silly. I can't eat all this."

"I'm sure he's planning to help you."

She smiled and set the box in her lap, stretching her legs, toes pointed. "You're probably right. I should take them with me skating, which reminds me..." She drew her legs in, glanced at her watch, put the lid back on the box, and got up. "I'd better get dressed."

She went first to the large vase of roses standing on the side table in front of the window and buried her face in their lush red blossoms, then turned away. It was almost a pirouette, that enormous candy box clutched to her chest. Owen wanted to shake her, but his assigned role in this farce was that of observer, and he intended to stick to it. He merely moved aside as she swept out into the foyer and poised on the bottom step of the stairway before starting up. Suddenly she stopped.

"Oh, I forgot. I won't be home for dinner. We're going out for a bite after the skating."

Now that was the straw that broke the camel's back. He tried so hard not to raise his voice, but sometimes he just couldn't help himself. "For Pete's sake, Bonnie, why didn't you say something earlier? I've made beef pies!"

She bit her lip apologetically, looking contrite. "Well, if you wouldn't mind, we could come back here to eat."

He couldn't believe this. He was positively agape over this. "You want *me* to serve you and the doctor a late supper?"

"Don't be silly," she said lightly. "I'll do it if you'll just stick a couple of extra pies in the fridge for us."

He folded his arms, struggling mightily to maintain a calm. The acidity he could not help. "I don't have a couple of *extra* pies. I have pies for our guests and for myself and for you. I wasn't expecting Steve Clark for dinner."

She shrugged, smiling. "Okay. Then I guess I'll just have my yummy pie for lunch tomorrow."

As if that made it all right! He ground his teeth as she skipped up the stairs, along the landing, and into her room. He wanted to throw things and shout and demand that she stop acting like a lovesick kid. She was young, but she wasn't sixteen anymore. And Clark was no better. What kind of doctor sent four pounds of cholesterol-laden chocolates to a patient? He made himself relax and go downstairs to remind their half a dozen guests that dinner would be served at six. This, too, was an exercise in self-control because he had to talk over the zing-zing-zap of the video game.

He hated that thing. Truth be told, he never had liked it, but their guests seemed to be crazy about it. He couldn't understand why. He'd tried his hand at it a few times, but the fascination that it seemed to hold for others eluded him. He thought it was an infantile pastime, and it *wasn't* just because Steven Clark had beaten him at a game one night two weeks earlier. Of course, he hated losing. He was honest enough to admit that. But he didn't hate Steven Clark. He just didn't wholly approve of the man's recent behavior.

For instance, what kind of a doctor neglected his patients in order to spend time with some woman? After all, weren't doctors supposed to be on call every moment of the day and night? Weren't they the most overworked professionals on the face of the earth? Weren't they supposed to be dedicated to providing the very best possible care to the ill? If so, then somebody ought to report this character for failing in the performance of his duty, because nobody who spent that much time making goo-goo eyes at some woman could be taking care of business!

Why, over the past month Steve Clark has probably spent more time at this place than at his own home, and Owen was getting darn tired of having him underfoot all the time. He'd have spoken to Bonnie about it, but he didn't want her to think he was trying to tell her who to date. No, sir. That was not it at all. Bonnie could date whomever she pleased. Bonnie *should* date. It just galled Owen no end that they had to be so damned immature about it. High school kids had to spend every available moment together. Adults had other things to do, important things to do. What was wrong with the doc, anyway? Who ever heard of a grown man taking a grown woman skating? And on the very occasion he was serving homemade beef pies, too. It was so frustrating to do all the work because somebody liked something and then have that somebody skip out at the last minute.

He wanted to hit things, but that would have been a dead giveaway, and he knew Bonnie would jump to all kinds of unwarranted conclusions if he gave in to his feelings of anger. Besides, he was an adult, and real adults controlled themselves. Real adults curtailed their impulses. And that was all he wanted Steve and Bonnie to do. Why couldn't they just cool it before something awful happened, something he couldn't name, something he didn't even want to think about, something... tragic. If he could feel it coming, why couldn't they? It was a question without an answer. Resigned, he went to the kitchen and savagely hacked up a trio of melons to serve with the beef pies. It was the best he could do when he wanted to do the worst.

Chapter Nine

Bonnie brushed her hair with long, strong strokes, parted it in the middle, and flipped her bangs forward, then picked up the fluffy wedding cake hat and tugged it down over her head. A few minor adjustments later, it snugly covered her ears and framed her face with a delicate fringe of white fur. She gave herself a critical once-over in the mirror. Skinny navy blue stretch pants with arch straps molded her lower body from thigh to waist. The matching turtleneck sweater fit more loosely, its hem just skimming the tops of her hips. She was trim and taut, one of the advantages of running up and down a flight of stairs many times a day. That, coupled with her habit of working with the small free weights she kept under her bed, kept her looking fit. She really did want to look her best. Steve had been so sweet.

She'd forgotten how much fun it was to be courted, and Dr. Steven Clark was one of the most romantic, sentimental men she had ever met. And yet she doubted that he was capable of the kind of deep, consuming emotion that was both Owen's strength and weakness.

Thoughts of Owen dulled her happy mood. Sighing, she spun and dropped onto the edge of the bed, reaching for the white fur muff that went with the hat. She could admit that she'd hoped Owen would be jealous, but it seemed that was not so. Oh, he was irritable a lot, but when wasn't he? No, the most she could hope for with Steve was that she could distract herself from thinking about Owen every waking moment. She smiled, thinking about the suave doctor. He could be such fun, and he tried so hard to charm her. He would never know how grateful she was for that.

She heard a strange honking sound rather like that of a goose and put away her troubled thoughts, wondering which of their neighbors had developed a fascination for barnyard fowl. A moment later, as she was hanging the muff about her neck by its knitted string, Owen bawled out her name. Perplexed, she grabbed the long, white fake fur coat, threw it about her shoulders, snatched up her skates, and went out. With both hands on the banister, she leaned over the landing railing and asked what was the matter. Owen walked to the parlor side of the foyer so he could see her and brought both hands to his hips.

"I've got dinner to serve," he said. "Would you kindly greet your own date?"

It was then that Steve joined him, looking a little sheepish in his gray wool coat, a red muffler wound about his throat. "I'm early," he said apologetically. "These things are faster than I assumed."

She smiled at him. "What things?"

He smiled back. "Come and see."

Intrigued, she walked around the landing and descended the stairs, her fingers trailing along the banister. Steven moved to the door as she walked toward him, opening it as she drew near. With a flourish, he directed her attention to the street. There waited a sleigh, red, with great scrolled fenders, a lantern suspended in the crook of each. A middle-aged gentleman stood beside it, wearing a leather cap with earflaps and a plaid lumberjack's coat. In his hands he held the reins to a large, woolly, dappled horse that snuffled puffs of breath into the frigid air. As if sensing their presence, the horse swung his shaggy head, belled harness jingling merrily.

Bonnie laughed. "Steven, how wonderful!"

"Happy Valentine's," he said. "I wanted it to be a special evening."

"Do you suppose we'll be warm enough?" she asked, turning her back to him so he could lift the coat from her shoulders and hold it while she slipped her arms into the sleeves, switching the skates from hand to hand.

He chuckled softly and settled the coat, smoothing her long, dark hair over the snowy fur. "We'll snuggle," he promised, and the sound of his voice was so warm and intimate that she blushed, keenly aware of Owen standing just to one side. She glanced at him, saw the black scowl on his face, and looked away.

"I thought you were going skating," Owen muttered.

"I thought you had to serve dinner," Steven returned smoothly.

"That's right," Owen came back, moving across the foyer. "I have to do just about everything around here."

Bonnie felt a sharp stab of guilt. Normally she would be around to help serve dinner and clean up. She turned toward Owen, apology on her face. "I hope you don't mind."

Immediately he looked contrite. "Go on," he said. "Get out from underfoot. It does you good to get out of the house."

"It does you good, too," she reminded him. He shrugged, and his eyes went to Steven. There was enough malevolence in that look to shock Bonnie and then to send a shiver down her spine, but the next instant he had turned away and walked into the dining room. What was that she had just seen? she wondered. Was it possible that his irritability stemmed from jealousy after all? "Good night," she called after him hopefully.

"Don't wait up!" Steven added.

If Owen made a reply, they didn't hear it. Steven shrugged and placed his hand against the small of her back. They went out the door, across the porch, down the steps, along the walk, and through the picket gate to the street. Their driver greeted them and climbed up onto his seat. Steve helped her inside the open sleigh and settled down beside her. A heavy gray blanket was folded over the seat facing them. He took it, shook it out, and tossed it over their legs before putting his arm around her. He drew her close and tucked the blanket in tight.

"Warm enough?" he asked, and she nodded, smiling uncomfortably and feeling her gaze wander back to the house. It was then that she spied Owen's powerful form in the dining-room window.

His hands were clasped behind him, and his head was bowed, but she had no doubt that he was watching. Her heart gave a pronounced thump. Instinctively she moved away from Steven a bit, but his arm tightened about her reflexively, reminding her that she was his date and not Owen's. She managed a self-conscious smile as the driver flipped the reins and clucked his tongue. They moved forward with a slight lurch. Bonnie turned her head for a last look and came right up against Steven's profile. Steven, not Owen. It was unreasonable, of course, to feel such keen disappointment, such sharp longing, but one thing Bonnie had learned was that feelings could not always be controlled. She reminded herself that behavior was something else again and forced new brightness into her smile. Steven settled her more comfortably in the fold of his arm before turning his eyes forward, but Bonnie could only fight the urge to look back and stiffen her smile, while her enthusiasm for this evening went suddenly limp.

Owen turned away from the sink, frowning. He couldn't bring himself to finish the cleaning, and he didn't want to play pool or shut himself away with a book. The music that played on the stereo in the parlor grated on his nerves like nails on a chalkboard, and every distant pop and bang of the gun battle being portrayed on the television downstairs seemed to penetrate his skull. But it was none of these things that made him abandon the kitchen, fish his skates out of the front closet, put on his coat, and walk out the back door, leaving dirty dishes, tenants, and his good judgment behind him. It was the way Steven Clark had spoken to Bonnie, the subtle messages about this being a special evening for the two of them, his arm pulling her close in the back seat of that sleigh, his whole damned proprietary manner, as if she belonged to him—or soon would. It wasn't any of his business, of course, and he knew Bonnie was a savvy lady who could take care of herself, but he just couldn't stand and stare any longer, wondering what they were doing and how they were doing it. Besides, he needed to get out once in a while, too. Bonnie herself had said as much earlier.

As he was backing the truck out into the street, he realized that they might not have gone skating, after all. In fact, they could be anywhere by now, anywhere at all, even in Steve's neat, angular little house out on Lake County Road. He'd check the ice rink first, and if they weren't there . . .

He didn't want to think about what he was going to do if they weren't there. He didn't want to think about them not being there. He didn't want to think about it at all.

The front of the house was dark when Bonnie stepped up onto the porch. She laughed as Steven commented again about the little girl who'd bitten into the barrel of an ink pen and colored her mouth, lips, and chin a dark, splotchy blue. He'd been telling the story in snippets all evening. It seemed that the child's mother had feared she had swallowed enough ink to poison herself and had snatched up the girl and rushed her to the emergency room without coat or shoes. By the time Steven had arrived on the scene, half the nurses, the examining table, and the mother's sweater, in which she'd wrapped the child, were smudged and stained. Judging from the amount of ink he saw and the mess in the little girl's mouth, he doubted that she'd been able to ingest enough to cause a toxic reaction, but she was going to be wearing some strange-looking ink splotches for some time to come. Bonnie could well imagine the child's face and the mother's consternation, but that wasn't what made her laugh.

What made her laugh was the thought of Owen skating out onto the ice that coated what was in winter months an ice rink and in summer tennis courts. He skated well enough, but he was such a big man that he stuck out like a sore thumb among all those children and even the few adults. Steven had openly gaped, but she had been thrilled to see him, hoping against hope that she was the reason he had come. Even now she couldn't say with certainty that this was so. He hadn't asked her to skate with him, and he hadn't spent a great deal of time chatting, either, but she had sensed his eyes upon her more than once, and the way he'd offered to save Steven the trouble of taking her home had hinted at something other than mere politeness.

She had been sorry to remind him that they were going for dinner and had hoped Steve wasn't going to make too big a production of it. Fortunately he had not. The sleigh had dropped them off at the ice rink, where Steve's car had been parked, and gone on its way, so after skating they'd driven to a local Mexican restaurant and shared *fajitas* for two. Steve had been disappointed when she'd turned down his offer for drinks at his place but had taken her rebuff in stride with his usual good humor. She truly liked Steve, and she enjoyed his company, but how could she allow herself to get into a potentially passionate situation with him when she yearned for some sign from Owen that he cared? Early on, she had given Steve to understand that a physical relationship was out of the question, but he had likewise given her to understand that he was going to try to change her mind. That had seemed fair enough then; now, when all she could think about was whether or not Owen was jealous, it seemed unkind at best. Was it wicked of her to hope that Owen was just a little jealous? She decided it was, but just the prospect of such a thing made her so happy that she couldn't help hoping.

Steve opened the front door and stood aside as she went in. The house felt warm and toasty. Bonnie dropped her skates, then slid her coat off and draped it over the banister. A light shone from the back of the foyer, testifying that the light was on in the reception room downstairs. It cast the foyer into shadows. Steven closed the door and came to stand beside her, his hand settling in the small of her back again. Without the added thickness of her coat beneath it, his touch felt overly familiar. She knew he hoped to be asked to stay for a while, but she wanted him to go. She wanted him not to touch her. Still, he had been so dear, so very attentive, and a real gentleman.

She turned to him, saying, "I'm exhausted!" and moving his hand from her back to her elbow.

Steve chuckled. "How many times," he asked, "do you suppose we went around that rink?" As he spoke, he drew her to him, and it was all she could do not to skip away. Instead, she put both hands against his chest and tried to smile.

"A hundred, at least!"

"Several hundred," he murmured, leaning toward her.

She felt his cool lips against hers and relaxed, finding it not unpleasant, but kept her hand planted firmly against his chest, a reminder of their understanding. He didn't get the hint. His arms came up and around her and pulled her close. She tensed, but before she could even begin to push away, the overhead light came on. They broke apart, the brightness blinding after the near darkness.

"Sorry about that," said a deep voice from the vicinity of the dining room.

Owen.

Bonnie smiled, all but laughing outright, as Steven stammered that it was a-a-all right. "Yes," she said, taking up her coat again. "It's late anyway, and Steve was just about to go." Steven frowned, but she ushered him to the door, smiling all the while. "Thank you so much for a lovely, memorable evening, and thank you again for the flowers and the chocolates and the sleigh ride. It was all such fun." She let him out and kissed him quickly on the cheek, saying, "Good night." Reluctantly he went across the porch and down the steps. Bonnie closed the door and whirled.

Owen slipped his hands into his pockets and stepped into the room, his jaw working back and forth. "Things seem to be getting serious between you and the doc," he said.

She shook her head, thrilled to the bottom of her feet. "It was just a good-night kiss."

His dark brow hitched up, but he said nothing else.

After a few moments of uncomfortable silence, she gave her hand a flutter and shrugged. "Well, I guess I'll go on up."

He nodded, but even as she moved toward the stairs, he spoke. "You looked like a kid out there tonight."

"But I'm not," she told him brightly, stopping to turn on one of the lower steps.

He rubbed the back of his neck. "You're a lot closer to it than I am."

"Oh, I don't know about that," she said, grinning happily. "Didn't anybody tell you? It's all a state of mind."

He shrugged. "Maybe. Anyway, I'm sorry for breaking up your date."

"No problem." She waited for him to speak again, and just when it seemed he wasn't going to, he did.

"Listen," he said, "I think I owe you another apology. I've been a real grouch lately, and I'm sorry about that, too." He squinted up at her and then suddenly looked away, as if regretting that he'd spoken.

Bonnie wanted to hug him and tell him it was all right, but she knew she couldn't do that. Instead, she placed both hands on the railing and leaned forward slightly. "When are you going to get it through your head," she asked him, "that I like you just the way you are?"

He looked at her, and then he smiled rather self-consciously. "Good night," he said, just that and nothing more. Somehow it was enough.

"Good night."

She went up without looking back, but she knew he was watching, and she was glad.

Life was downright pleasant. Owen couldn't have said what had happened. He only knew that he liked being with her. He couldn't seem to help himself, especially when she smiled, and she seemed to be doing a lot of that lately. She smiled when she came down for coffee in the morning, and she smiled when she said good-night for the evening. She had even smiled when he'd let the omelet stick to the pan and made a mess of their lunch, and now she was smiling because he'd suggested they take advantage of this lull in the schedule to get in a few hours of fun while they could.

"I'll change and grab my skis," she said, practically skipping with glee as she left the room.

He leaned back in his chair and grinned at the remains of the ruined omelet. Yes, indeed, life could be good. Bookings were rolling in for the month of March from all over Texas. Those Lone Star Staters were so hot to ski, they'd probably melt the snow on their way down the mountain. In fact, it seemed half the population of the state was going to be up on the mountain on any given day during the Spring Break season. The lodge was already booked full for two whole weeks, and calls were still coming in. Bonnie's advertising campaign had paid off in a big way. She deserved a day out. She deserved more than that, but more than that he felt unable to provide. And yet, he was beginning to wonder if he didn't underestimate them both.

He couldn't help smiling when he remembered what she'd said to him on the evening of Valentine's Day. No other woman had ever told him that she liked him just as he was. Tish certainly hadn't. From the beginning she had been more interested in making him over than learning to love him just as he was, while he had tried alternately to fit her idea of who and what he should be and trust that she would come to appreciate the real him. But then he was mixing apples and oranges again. He and Bonnie were friends and business partners, not lovers, and he intended to keep it that way. *So why,* he asked himself, *did you sabotage Steve Clark's good-night kiss?*

The short answer was, of course, that he was afraid to touch her himself but didn't want anyone else to. However, he mulled it around for some time before he came to that, and even then he tried to soften the proof of his own feelings for the woman by telling himself that Dr. Steven Clark was the wrong man for Bonnie Maxwell and that as her friend, he, Owen, owed it to her not to let her make a mistake. He was honest enough to admit to himself that he liked being around her. She made him feel young again and...vulnerable. In other words, she also scared the hell out of him, and though he kept telling himself that he simply could not allow himself to fall in love with her, he had started to wonder if perhaps he really could. Bonnie was not Tish, after all. How did he know it wouldn't work out between them if he really tried? Then he remembered that he'd thought the same thing with Tish, and the deep hurt of that experience seemed to overwhelm him once more. Then he knew that it all boiled down to whether or not he was willing to take a chance, and he wasn't. But that didn't mean he couldn't enjoy her company, did it?

Bonnie came in wearing her ski suit and a smile as wide as Texas, and he stopped thinking about whether he could enjoy her company and just did.

She said, "You're not ready."

Instantly he got up and crumpled his napkin over his plate and the remains of the bungled omelet. He felt himself grin, and knew he shouldn't feel so good just looking at her but couldn't help it. "Get the gear in the truck," he said. "I'll be along in a minute."

She nodded happily and went out again, heading for the big closet in the foyer. He went quickly through the kitchen, down the hall, and into his room. He got into the proper clothing, zipped his wallet into an inside pocket, and snatched the truck keys off the desk. A moment later he stuck his head out the back door. She was there, waiting. Two pairs of skis and boots and two snowboards were waiting, too. He punched his hands into gloves and went out to buckle down the protective cover of the truck bed. He got into the truck and fit his key into the ignition.

"This is going to be fun," she said, and into his mind came the thought, *If I let it*. He realized suddenly that it was up to him, and for some reason that alarmed him. Then an intense and immediate feeling of shame overcame him. He wasn't such a coward that he couldn't even let Bonnie enjoy herself, was he? He pumped up his smile and put the transmission in gear.

"You're due a little fun," he told her.

"We both are," she insisted as he backed the truck out into the street. "We've both worked hard, and this partnership has been quite an adjustment for each of us in our separate ways. I think we ought to treat ourselves better, frankly."

"I think you may be right," he agreed, heading the truck toward Harrison Avenue. "What did you have in mind?"

She crossed her long, slender legs and seemed to think this through. "I've been meaning to start a regular workout at the gym. You know, for a small fee we could even guarantee our guests full use of the facilities. It would be worth it just for our own use, though. I mean, if you're interested in jogging and weight lifting and the occasional basketball game."

He chuckled. "So the lady plays basketball, too, does she?"

She lifted her shoulders in a resigned shrug. "Okay, so you could probably beat me with one hand tied behind your back."

"I didn't say that!" he protested.

"Well, even if you could," she went on, "it'd still be fun. Wouldn't it?"

"Yeah," he said softly, "it would," and he meant it.

"So should we do it? Should we book an hour at the gym?"

For a moment he felt that old reflex, the tightening of his hand on the steering wheel, the stiffening of his muscles, the automatic pulling back. The fact that he wanted to do this with her didn't mean anything. His gut reaction was the same. He wanted to see her moves on a basketball court. He wanted to hear her laugh as she beat him to the line or got brought up short. He wanted to beat her fair and square and listen to her kid him about his lay-up, make a smooth three-pointer, and let her marvel at his style.

So why the hell couldn't he just do it? He decided that he would. For once, he made an instant decision without worrying about getting too close or being misunderstood or winding up hurt somewhere down the line, and it felt good just not to fear getting hurt for a while.

"Sure," he said as casually as he could manage. "Why not?"

She flipped him a thumbs-up sign, grinning like a kid with a new toy, and he felt himself following suit, pleased because she was pleased. A part of him cowered, but another part of him was glad, and it superseded the other. It wasn't so hard to just enjoy being with her, after all. In fact, it was surprisingly easy. He settled back behind the wheel and let himself consider what it would be like to maintain this state of affairs indefinitely.

They reached the ski area in short order and wasted no time getting out on the slopes. It was only the two of them this day, and that proved to be an easy, workable situation. They concentrated on the snowboards most of the time. Bonnie wanted to improve her form, and Owen had enough experience to be of real help. She was amazing. She learned quickly and had real athletic ability, but she didn't hurt his feelings any when she insisted her progress was due to his "invaluable" coaching.

When the slopes closed they went home, changed, took a dozen messages off of the answering machine, divided them up to be dealt with the next day, and started dinner, after which they watched a made-for-television movie on the big screen downstairs and went separately to bed.

He shouldn't have been surprised when she informed him bright and early the next morning that they would be going to the gym at three o'clock, but he was, and he wavered back and forth during the day, wondering what he was going to do, if he was going to go, if it could possibly be as easy today as it had been yesterday to merely enjoy himself. At two-thirty she came and knocked on his bedroom door to tell him it was time to get their gear together for their workout. He started to make an excuse about needing to stay with the books in which he was making entries, but when he looked her way, his hand somehow picked up a side of the book and folded it closed. She smiled at him from the door and went away. He looked down at the closed accounts ledger, waiting for that moment of deep uncertainty, of pulling away, of closing in. It didn't come. Instead, he found himself wondering if she was going to play ball like a girl or if she could manage a real fadeaway jump shot. He got up and found a pair of shorts and a T-shirt suitable for basketball, then dug out his athletic shoes and white socks, a bathing suit, a towel and, finally, a bag to put it all in.

As it turned out, she could, indeed, manage a decent fadeaway, but he beat her handily, anyway. Of course, afterward she went on to run a mile and a half while he struggled to get a decent breath and stretch out a muscle cramp in his upper thigh. But when she finally joined him again, she was puffing even harder than he had been, and when he suggested a swim, she quickly refused, saying she was so tired she'd probably drown.

"But," she said, wiping sweat out of her eyes, "I'll take a rain check. We'll forget the basketball next time, and I'll show you how a real athlete laps the pool."

"In your dreams," he came back, rising effortlessly to the challenge. "I'll show you how it's done."

"Say when, hotshot."

He heard the word falling out of his mouth and marveled at the ease of it. "Tomorrow."

"You're on." She grinned and got up, swaggering toward the dressing room.

She was some sight, not that she'd dressed provocatively. Quite the opposite, in fact. The dingy white T-shirt she wore had a rip in one sleeve, and the combination of neon green spandex thigh-huggers paired with bright orange parachute shorts could hardly be called tantalizing. Her hair had started out in a neat ponytail augmented by a stretchy blue headband, but now it was falling down around her face in tendrils, the headband was askew, and the ponytail itself was sagging dangerously. In addition, her athletic shoes were designed for maximum shock absorption, giving them a clunky, overlarge look. Yet, she was beautiful. Every muscle in her body was trim and toned. Her shape was perfectly proportioned. She moved with incredible grace, clunky shoes and all. Her hair was glossy and sleek. And her face... Her face was perfect in every detail, from the dark, wispy brows arching over those sparkling light gray eyes to the straight line of a slightly tip-tilted nose and that lush, full-lipped mouth that smiled with such ease. He felt a sudden, fierce proudness for this woman and, with it, the deepest stirrings of desire. It was enough to make him rethink.

He told himself that evening, alone in his bed, that he would find a way out of tomorrow's swimming date, but with morning came that smile on that perfect face, and the afternoon found him stroking like a windmill in a gale in a losing attempt to outswim her. After that, she accused him of being a sore loser, to which he quipped that he was merely sore. She suggested something less strenuous for the next day's agenda, like a movie, then before he even had a chance to hedge, waxed enthusiastic about a "vintage" movie, something they hadn't seen but should have, one of the old greats, the classics. They gabbed about it for a while and decided on the 1948 Laurence Olivier version of *Hamlet*, simply because anything based upon a William Shakespeare play had to be a classic and Bonnie had noticed it in a local video rental store.

So it was on the last peaceful evening before the Spring Break onslaught, Owen found himself sitting beside Bonnie on the couch in the rec room, half-listening to the "Melancholy Dane" agonize on big-screen TV. His arm had somehow wound up draped about her shoulders, and he was looking not at the screen but at her charming profile when she turned her head to smile in his direction and their gazes bumped up against one another, paused, and suddenly zeroed in, like the close-up lens of a camera. Hamlet ceased to be.

Owen's needs hit him like a hammer blow. He was still reeling from the shock and already his arm was folding her close. Her head fell back gently against his bicep. The lids of her eyes slowly descended with a graceful sweep of long, thick black lashes. Her lips parted expectantly, compelling him to crush her mouth beneath his.

He pulled her closer, feeling her weight roll to his side, and plumbed the depths of her mouth with his tongue. Her arms went around his neck. It was not enough. He stretched out and shifted onto his side, pressing her against him. She responded with a slow undulation that hardened his groin and made his breath come in fast through his nostrils. He had to move, to make her body fit his. Their legs tangled. He reached down and pulled hers up out of the way. It curled about him, her body shifting against his, sliding slightly downward, and at the same time her tongue came up into his mouth, small and velvety and energetic. His need to fill her surged. He pushed her tongue away with his own, desperate now, and followed it back into the wet cavern of her mouth. The impetus seemed to carry them both downward.

She twisted and sank down onto her back, keeping that one leg wrapped about him, bringing the other up and bracing her foot against the cushion. His mouth never leaving hers, he crawled atop her, moving his body with hers until he lay between her legs, his feet hanging off the end of the couch, arms braced on either side of her upper torso. It was a shocking and wonderful place to be, seeming at once wholly natural and impossibly new.

She felt strong and vital beneath him, her slender body accommodating his heavy bulk and breadth within the narrow confines of the couch. He was struck with the happy realization that she was his to feel, taste, and explore, and pulled his tongue from her mouth in order to do just that, working his way along her jaw and beneath it. She rotated her head, allowing him access to the smooth column of her throat, and as he kissed the tender flesh, he felt her breath begin to speed, her chest rising and falling, her breasts thrusting and softening as she gasped and sighed and gasped. She wore a soft gold sweater with a wide ribbed collar that clung to the tops of her shoulders. With one hand he pushed it away, discovering no bra beneath, and revealed the luscious mounds of her breasts, full and firm and pink-tipped. He wanted to taste them and eased himself up onto his elbows, bending his head to capture first one peaked nipple and then the other.

When he tugged the first into his mouth, she cried out softly, a single syllable of intense pleasure. When he moved to the second, she twined the other leg about him, teasing the bend of his knee with her foot. He shifted his weight to one elbow, and slid the opposite hand downward, finding the elasticized waistband of her soft knit pants. He slipped his fingers beneath, down and across the rounded jut of her hipbone to the silky fabric of bikini briefs. He had every intention of going farther, of stoking her need, of stripping her bare, of joining their bodies in the most substantial manner possible, of sating this electrifying desire, but then she gripped his wrist firmly, unmistakably.

"Bonnie," he whispered against the satin of her skin, desperate, "let me make love to you."

Her free hand stroked his hair and skimmed his shoulder, but all the while she maintained her surprisingly steely grip. Finally she answered him. "No," she said regretfully but without any possibility of misunderstanding.

He felt, quite literally, as if he might cry, but he took his hand away and fortified himself with a deep breath, turning his face upward into the bend of her neck.

She turned her cheek down and laid it against the top of his head. "I want to make love with you, Owen," she told him softly, "but more than that, I want you not to regret it afterward."

Oh, the wisdom of this woman, the damnable, wonderful wisdom of her. It was enough to make him push his arms around her, to bring his cheek against hers, to hold her so tightly that he trembled with the effort of it. Steve Clark could love her without regret, but he could not. The knowledge was humbling, painful, bitter. He made himself release her, get up, sit, while she quietly righted her clothing and smoothed her hair.

"I'm sorry," he told her raggedly, not looking at her. "I try not to want you."

"I know," she said. "That's why I can't do it."

He nodded and leaned forward, putting his head into his hands. After a moment, she stood. He could feel her there, looming over him, a silent, gentle shadow, a beautiful dream. Then she bade him a quiet good-night and left him. He listened to her go, then sat back and tried to see the flickering images on the big screen. Hamlet did not agonize alone, but in the end he knew as much about his companion as his companion did of him.

Chapter Ten

They were inundated. For three weeks, thanks to Bonnie's Texas advertising campaign, every bed in the place was filled every night. There were enough people coming and going mornings and evenings to make the place look like Grand Central Station at rush hour and enough cash piling up to see the business safely through to the fall. The place was so busy that Bonnie couldn't keep up with the laundry and the cleaning, so Owen had to help her, despite his initial unease and his kitchen duties. But Bonnie was nothing if not forgiving. She said no word about what had happened—or almost happened—on the couch in the recreation room. Indeed, she was her usual calm, smiling self. Owen only wished that he could be as relaxed and self-possessed as she was. He could not help tensing when she came near or control the racing of his pulse whenever a look or a word or a certain motion brought back to him the memory of holding her, kissing her, caressing her.

Waking or sleeping, he could not forget how she had felt, tasted, looked. He remembered everything in depressing detail, every sound, touch, smell, flavor. And when he remembered, he ached. He seemed to be living in a constant state of arousal, which was why he couldn't trust himself to spend time with her unless it was filled with work. Fortunately he had plenty to do, as did Bonnie. That was why he didn't think too much about her not seeing Steve Clark during that time. He knew Steve called her because more times than not he was the one to answer the phone, but he naturally assumed that the heavy work load was the reason Steve didn't come around and Bonnie didn't go out to see him. As far as Owen was concerned, that was one of the benefits of all this activity, just one more way in which Bonnie's advertising scheme had paid off. Only after the rush for the slopes slowed to a trickle in the last week of March did he find out the truth.

It was one of those flukes, an accident, pure and simple. He was working on a leaky shower head downstairs when he remembered that he'd forgotten to leave the outgoing mail for the postman to pick up. Wrench and all, he hurried upstairs to his bedroom and snatched up the bundle of utility payments and query answers. He was passing through the foyer, heading for the mailbox set on a pole beside the gate in the front yard, when he heard Steve Clark's voice coming from the parlor.

"Can't we even have dinner together?" he was saying, and Owen immediately halted, piqued by Steve's mere presence. He meant only to steel himself, to tamp down his surge of envy and anger, but Bonnie's reply made him linger, ears pricked with intense interest.

"I'm sorry, Steve," she said, "but I don't think that would be wise."

Owen's brows went up in surprise. Thoughtlessly, he stepped closer to the parlor wall, the better to hear.

"I thought you enjoyed going out with me," Steve argued calmly. *So did I,* Owen concurred. Bonnie made it unanimous.

"Oh, I did! I do! I just don't think it's fair to go on seeing you, that's all."

"Fair?" Steven echoed. "Look, Bonnie, I know you don't feel for me quite what I feel for you, but that's all right. I don't mind—too much."

Owen cocked his head to one side, fully intrigued now, and imagined the scene beyond that wall. Steve was probably sitting on the edge of his chair, leaning forward tensely, feet planted flat upon the floor, while Bonnie occupied hers with ease and natural elegance, her long legs crossed casually at the knee. He could hear her composure in her voice.

"That's sweet of you to say," she told Steve, "but there's a little more to it than that, I'm afraid."

Steven sighed. "Is it Owen?" he asked, and the object of his question stiffened with confusion, and then she answered.

"Yes."

He was stunned and thrilled and appalled. He lifted a hand to his head, realized it held a wrench and let it fall absently at his side. Steve was saying that he'd suspected Owen was more to her than a business partner, even though she'd indicated otherwise.

"I didn't mean to mislead you," she said gently. "I felt it was hopeless before, and even now I can't be sure that my feelings are returned, but I love him, and so I can't very well go on seeing you, can I?"

Owen swayed against the wall. She loved him! Or thought she did. And after everything he'd said and done.

Then why, when he'd pressed her to make love with him, had she refused? He closed his eyes and let it all happen again, his arm about her shoulders, his mouth on hers, that leg curling about him as he bore her down. *I want to make love to you, Owen, but more than that I want you not to regret it.* Not to regret it. She had done it for his sake, because of his uncertainty. What was that, he asked himself, if not love? That sweet kid. What was he going to do with her?

He realized suddenly that Steve was leaving and knew he should beat a hasty retreat, but couldn't make himself move. They walked into the foyer and to the door. Steve was saying that he would miss her when she seemed to sense Owen's presence and half turned to glance over her shoulder. He saw the flash of recognition in her eyes and the instant certainty, but she turned back to Steve with that incredible aplomb, no hint in her manner that Owen was there. Steve kissed her cheek and let himself out of the door without ever knowing that Owen watched. Bonnie closed it behind him, folded her hands, and put her back to it.

"You heard?" It was as much statement as question. Owen nodded, shoulders lifting in an expression of apology.

"I couldn't help it. I was taking the mail out and..." How to explain that instant of jealousy, the surprise that had held him there?

"It's just as well," she said. "I was going to tell you, anyway."

"Were you?" he asked. "All of it?"

For the first time her serene composure faltered. She glanced away, biting her lip, then back again. "Maybe not quite in that manner."

They both looked away then, each knowing what the other was thinking. Owen shifted his weight and caught a fresh breath. "I don't know what to say," he told her honestly. She nodded in understanding.

"Neither do I."

But something had to be said. They couldn't leave it like this, and they both knew it.

"Let's sit down," he suggested, and she nodded once more, before moving forward into the parlor. He followed her, laying the wrench and mail on the lamp table. She chose the rocker nearest the easy chair and sat down. He took the easy chair, leaned forward with hands on knees, realized that was precisely the position he'd imagined for Steve, and got up again, rubbing the back of his neck.

"I've been trying to think how to do this for weeks," she began, her voice trembling nervously. "I keep telling myself that if I don't do it, I'll have to leave soon, but I'm just not sure, you see? So I keep putting it off. I guess it's a good thing you overheard. Now I have to do it, don't I?"

He was confused. He'd heard her say that she loved him and that she wouldn't see Steve Clark anymore because of it, but what was this thing she had to do? He asked her. She looked down at her hands, so uncharacteristically shaken that he wanted to go and put his arms around her and tell her everything was going to be all right. He didn't, of course. He didn't dare.

"I can't go on and on this way, Owen," she said softly. "The lodge doesn't matter anymore. Nothing does—except you."

He wanted so desperately to hold her, to let himself be elated by what she was saying, but he just didn't know how to do it. He'd held himself back for so long that he didn't know how to reach out. He tried to tell her that. "Bonnie, I don't—"

"Please, Owen," she interrupted. "Let me finish before you say anything." He nodded and turned away, trying to suppress the need to touch her. She went on. "I do believe, Owen, that you care for me, perhaps more than you're willing to admit even to yourself, and that's why I've been thinking, hoping... What I'm trying to say is that I love you—and I want you to marry me."

He couldn't have been more shocked if she'd shot him. He spun around, mouth agape, and stared at her. She put a crooked smile on her face, but her gaze was level and frank. She was serious. She was asking him to marry her! He felt suddenly as if his knees might buckle, and dropped down into the chair. It was a moment before he could find his voice.

"I had no idea you were thinking like this," he told her. "I can't believe you mean it."

"Why not?" she asked, cocking her pretty head to one side. "Surely you can see how I feel about you."

"I'm beginning to," he mumbled, "except... Marriage! Bonnie, I've been married! That's not something you do just because you think you love someone!"

"I don't think I love you," she came back calmly. "I *do* love you."

"You can't be sure!" he argued. "No one can! And feelings change, Bonnie, believe me."

"Of course they do," she said, "but that doesn't mean a marriage has to fail. If the commitment remains, you work your way through it, that's all, and anyway, change can be for the better, you know. Our feelings have changed just since I've been here! And look what a good team we've made, how well we've done. I know we could make it work, Owen. I know it!''

He pushed his hand through his hair. ''You're not thinking rationally,'' he told her raggedly. ''Marriage isn't a business deal!''

''I didn't say it was.''

''And love isn't enough, Bonnie! It takes hard work, harder than anything you've ever known!''

''I'm not afraid.''

''I am!'' He shot up out of his chair and strode away, but she wasn't about to let him off that easily. She got up and came after him, catching him in the foyer with a hand placed firmly on his shoulder. He turned, knowing he couldn't escape this, wishing to God that he could.

''I love you,'' she said, only that, and his arms went out and around her before he could stop them.

''Oh, Bonnie, it's not that I want to lose you, but what kind of husband would I be? You need someone who can trust you. You deserve that.''

''You'll learn,'' she insisted, her arms clamped about his waist.

''And children,'' he went on. ''You need a man young enough to help you raise a couple of kids.''

''I need you,'' she said, ''and don't forget that I was here at Christmastime. I watched you with your nieces. I know you'd be a wonderful father.''

''I'm too old to start a family!''

''Don't be silly,'' she said. ''Of course, if you really don't want children, I suppose I could live with that. I'd have to, wouldn't I? Since I love you so very much.''

''Bonnie!'' He was exasperated with her, but he hugged her close, afraid suddenly to let her go. ''Couldn't we just give this some time, see how we feel in a few months?''

"And till then?" she asked, pulling back to look up at him. "Owen, the season ends the first week in April. What am I supposed to do here after that? Eat chocolates, make love, and hope you'll suddenly develop an overwhelming need to visit a justice of the peace? Or am I supposed to believe that you'll be happy to hold hands with me indefinitely? Not that I don't want to make love with you."

"Then stay," he urged her, knowing she was right. "Or come back in the fall! We're partners, after all, and I'm going to need you when that horde from Texas comes pouring over the mountain. Then if we still feel the same..."

But she shook her head. "That's not enough anymore, Owen. I already know how I feel about you, what I want. I want to marry you, Owen. Isn't that proof of my feelings? Can't you just accept them and let us be happy together? Please?"

He wanted to. She would never know how much he wanted to. He had a fleeting vision of what it would be like to wake up beside her after a long night of passionate sex, to see her smile and welcome him to a new day. It didn't have to turn out like last time. She said she loved him, and that meant things would be different, didn't it?

He couldn't help it. The next thought just sneaked into his head and played itself out. Tish had said she loved him. She had said nothing but marriage would do for them, that she'd never leave him, that they'd be happy. He pulled his arms back and stepped away.

"I can't," he said quietly. "I'm sorry, I just can't."

Bonnie looked away. "Well," she said, her voice trembling again. "I guess that's that."

He felt like a snail, only lower. "Honey, please, try to understand."

"Oh, I do," she said quickly, moving toward the stairway. "I understand perfectly." She stopped on the bottom step and turned to face him. Her eyes glittered with unshed tears. "I took a shot—and I missed."

"Bonnie..." He moved forward, wanting very much to hold her again, but she shook her head.

"Uh-uh. If you do that, I'll cry, and I don't like women who..." Suddenly she turned and ran up the stairs.

This time she really didn't want to talk about it, but the silence that had served her so well in the months past seemed now to be an irritant to Owen. He tried. More than once, he tried. But outright rejection had finally been too much for Bonnie. She felt continually on the verge of tears, and though she exercised her smile as much as possible during that final week, her disappointment cloaked her like a heavy garment. She had known that she was taking a big chance when she proposed to Owen, but desperation can sometimes color possibilities with a decidedly rosy hue. She had only thought herself prepared for possible rejection. Now that it was reality, however, she had to cope with it, which meant, to her mind, protecting herself from the ever ready tears. If she attempted to talk about it, she would cry; hence, she could not talk about it.

She began to prepare herself for departure. They argued briefly over whether or not she ought to take with her those things she had bought for decoration or wait for him to reimburse her their cost. She didn't really care about the cost, but he was adamant, so she drew up a list of things she judged he could not really do without, and then they argued about whether he would reimburse her at their current value or original price. Reaching an accord at last, she began to pack.

It was difficult. Halfheartedly, she stripped the parlor of
vases, lamps, pillows, and pictures and packed them into
boxes, cushioned by crumpled newspapers. The drapes and
rug would stay. Next went the china, crystal, flatware, and
linens she had bought for Thanksgiving, followed by various items from the bedrooms. There was no question but
that the television and video game equipment would stay.
He insisted, however, that she take the VCR. Finally came
her sports gear and personal things. She packed everything except two changes of clothing and her toiletries and,
on the fifth day of April, loaded it all into her Suburban
while he was away from the house.

He had made it clear that he had no intention of helping
her pack, and she actually preferred it that way, but when
he came home and found that the boxes had been moved
from the foyer, he blew his stack. Suddenly they were
screaming at one another, recalling every ugly detail of the
partnership from the moment she'd arrived. She told him
he was stiff-necked and prideful. He called her a know-it-
all debutante who tried to buy accomplishment. She retal-
iated by labeling him ungrateful and spiteful and suspicious. He pointed out for the 672nd time that he had never
wanted a partner, and she told him in the deadly calm of
white hot anger that she was the best thing that had ever
happened to him and his lodge, but he was just too stupid
to know it. With that she locked herself away in her room.
He came up later and apologized through the door, but she
wouldn't open it to him. Later that evening, however, their
friends came by to say farewell, and she found that she
couldn't ignore them. She washed her face and went
downstairs, saying nothing whatsoever to Owen.

The Fergusons were there, of course, and Kim Nabob
and Jack Hampton and Celia Zimmer and her husband—

and Dr. Steven Clark. Steve was as long-faced as Owen himself and quite anxious to talk to her. They slipped out onto the front porch for a few minutes. Bonnie insisted, to his consternation, that nothing had changed. Despite the fact that she could have cheerfully broken the man's skull, she loved Owen. How could she see another man when her heart belonged to him? It made no difference that he did not return her feelings. Steve wondered if she'd change her mind in a few months, and she told him truthfully that she very much hoped so. He promised he'd call, but since she didn't know where she would be or what she would be doing, she gave him her parents' telephone number. When they went back inside, Bonnie noticed Owen glaring at the two of them from the easy chair in the parlor, but she ignored him. Anger made that easy, but there were other reasons. For one, she had misread so much of what Owen had done that she didn't trust herself to interpret his actions anymore. She concentrated on the friends she had made here, Owen's friends.

The Fergusons wanted her to say that she'd return to ski during the coming season, but she avoided making any ironclad promises. Kim Nabob announced that the young woman he was dating had relatives in Dallas and he had sort of promised he'd take her to visit them. Celia Zimmer said things were getting pretty serious when you started meeting relatives, and everybody hooted and teased him about this being "the one." He colored, but didn't deny he was thinking seriously.

"Well, I, for one, respect a man who isn't afraid to think seriously about a woman," Bonnie told him, then instantly regretted having spoken. Apparently nearly all those present had suspected that she possessed romantic feelings for her business partner, and she had just confirmed that they were unrequited. She felt ashamed, as ridiculous as that was, and it was pretty obvious that everyone else felt sorry for her, even Owen, who got up and mumbled something about beer in the refrigerator before making a hasty exit. Bonnie tried to deflect attention by inviting Kim and his girlfriend to visit her while they were in Dallas. "I don't know exactly where I'll be staying, but you can always reach me through my parents," she said, and she gave him their telephone number and address in Highland Park. He promised to look her up, and they discussed for a bit all the other things in Dallas that he ought to see while there.

Owen came in with bottles of cold beer and mugs, as well as a tray of sliced cheeses and crackers and crudités. Everyone seemed relieved for the distraction and partook with relish only slightly forced, but it soon became clear that no one was really in much of a party mood. Bonnie thanked them all for coming and put a merciful end to the evening by saying that she had a long drive awaiting her and needed to make a very early start in the morning. They filed out, one by one, wishing her well and encouraging her to return whenever possible. Steve stayed till the last, and despite Owen's scowling presence, kissed her full on the mouth and reminded her that he would be in touch. When they had all departed, she felt strangely exhausted. It had been, after all, a trying day, and tomorrow promised to be worse.

She started upstairs, supposing they'd said—or shouted—all there was to say, but when Owen called out to her, she found hope had not died at all and turned with her heart in her throat to stare down at him. He seemed to regret having spoken. Hope relinquished, and she turned, but suddenly he was bounding up the stairs after her. He stopped with one foot on a level with hers and the other on the next lower step, his palms rubbing nervously against his jeaned thighs.

"I want to tell you again," he said, "that I didn't mean any of those things I said today."

She nodded, gaze averted. "All right. Thank you. I didn't mean what I said, either. At least not all of it." She lifted her foot to take the next step and continue on with what was probably her last journey up these stairs, but he halted her again, this time with a hand clamped over her forearm.

"I've already told you that I don't want you to go," he said. "Couldn't we…negotiate?" She shook her head and climbed on, but he came with her. "I'll sign papers this time. Any terms you want."

"It isn't business any longer," she said quietly, and up the steps she went.

He let go of her, saying, "We've made such a good team!"

"Yes" was her simple reply. She reached the landing and turned toward her room, moving slowly and feeling as old as the house itself. It was nothing for him to run ahead and block the way.

"I won't touch you again," he promised, looking down at her with unusually bright eyes. "I swear to God, Bonnie, I won't lay a finger on you."

She smiled tiredly, looking up at him much as she'd done that first day, weary to the bone and a little awed by the sight of him, mountainous and all gold and silver with a dash of smoky black and the arresting blue-green of his eyes, bits of sky reflected in mossy pools. "Don't you see, Owen?" she said gently. "It wouldn't work. I want you to touch me and I don't know how to stop."

"Bonnie," he whispered, "I need you!"

Her smile widened temporarily. "So you do. And I need you, too, Owen, all of you, more than you can give me."

His hands hovered about her shoulders. He forced them down to his sides and licked his lips. "You have to understand," he said. "I don't know how to be in love."

"Yes, you do," she told him. "You were in love once. Don't you think I know that? Don't you think I can see it? You were in love and you were burned—bad—and now you wear the scars like armor."

"Maybe with time," he began, but she shook her head.

"I don't blame you," she said, lifting a hand to his cheek. "I don't want to get burned, either."

He seemed genuinely shaken but resigned. He dropped his gaze, breathed through his mouth, and swallowed. "I guess that's it then," he said, and she took her hand away.

"I guess it is."

He stepped back and then to the side. "Well..." He swallowed again and nodded. "Good night."

She let him get halfway down before she went to the railing and leaned over the side. "Owen," she called. He stopped and looked up, eyes gleaming in the foyer light. "Goodbye."

He was awake when she came down the stairs in the pre-dawn darkness. She stepped down into the foyer. Dully, he listened to the whispers of movement as she walked about. Then suddenly she appeared in the doorway of the parlor, a black shape against the gray of night receding in the emergence of day. His hand reflexively clutched the tall, slender glass within its grip. It had been empty for hours, but still he held it, his mind fogged by a haze of emotion. He had intended to get drunk, but he'd never been very good at mindless drinking, and eventually the ice in his single glass of scotch had melted and watered down the liquor. At some point he'd upended it, but had never gotten up to pour himself a refill. He wished he had a good stiff belt right then to help him endure what was coming, but then she turned and walked away, apparently failing to see him there in the shadows that cloaked the easy chair. He remembered having taken the bottle and glass from the cabinet, filling the glass with ice, pouring over the liquor, and carrying it all into the parlor to turn off the light before heading for his room, but he'd made it no farther than the easy chair.

He was tired, but that was to be expected, having sat up all night with an empty highball glass in hand. It had been a long time since he'd done something like this, more than five years, in fact. The thought was so depressing that he pushed it away, telling himself that he ought to get up and put on a pot of coffee. She'd need a good breakfast, too, and sitting across the table from her one more time would lend a bit of normalcy to this dreaded morning. He tried not to think that it would be the last time. With a sigh, he lifted his arm and moved the glass toward the lamp table, edging forward at the same time. It was then that he heard the door opening. For an instant, he couldn't believe that she could be going, then abruptly he was electrified and on his feet.

"Bonnie!"

She halted, the muted screech of the door hinges giving way to instant silence. He hurried into the foyer, seeing with eyes well adjusted to the dark the strip of thick gray light revealed by the opened door. Bonnie stood to one side just beyond the threshold, her hand on the doorknob, the bulk of her overnight bag balanced against her hip, its strap, no doubt, slung across her shoulder. He found the switch and flicked on the overhead light.

"You were going without saying goodbye?" He had to squint in the sudden brightness but saw enough to form an indelible impression. She wore a bulky red-and-white sweater and red knit pants. Her dark hair flowed over her shoulders to the middle of her back, held in place by a wide red headband that covered her ears.

"I didn't know you were there," she said softly, and moved back inside, gently closing the door. "Why didn't you say something?"

He hitched a shoulder in reply. "I thought you saw me."

She shook her head and looked down, biting her lip. Owen became aware of a vague ache in the small of his back and put his hands to it.

"Want some breakfast?" he asked, intuitively striving for a normal tone.

"No, thanks. I need to get on the road."

So much for normalcy. "Have some coffee, anyway," he urged, but she shook her head stubbornly.

"I meant to make this easy," she told him. "I said my goodbyes last night. I wanted to be gone before you were up this morning."

He was deeply, intensely offended. "You thought slipping out before daylight would make this easy?" he demanded. "Easy for whom? Certainly not for me!"

She sighed and slid the straps off her shoulder, letting the bag swing to the floor. "All right," she said. "It was the coward's way out. I'm sorry. But this isn't exactly painless either!"

"Whose fault is that! I'm not the one leaving!"

"Someone had to, because all we do is fight!"

"I don't *want* it that way!"

"Neither do I! But that's sure as hell how it is!"

"Fine!" he heard himself shout. "So go! Get out of here, if that's what you want!"

"It's not what I want," she told him shakily. "It's what has to be!" With that she yanked the door open and stomped out, dragging her bag behind her. He slapped it closed again with the flat of his hand, teeth clenched against an angry roar.

Damn the woman! Couldn't she see what this was doing to him? He felt as if he was ripping apart inside, as if his life had been gutted of everything pleasurable and worthwhile. Dear God, it was happening again, the very thing he'd tried to avoid. The woman he loved…loved him still. And he was letting her go!

It hit him like a ton of bricks. He shouldn't be letting her go. He should be binding her to him with every means at his disposal. She didn't even want to go! She wanted to marry him, for Pete's sake! She only wanted to know that he loved her as she loved him! What was wrong with him? He put both hands to his head, ready to tear out his hair, when he heard the low rumble of the Suburban's engine.

Wildly, unthinking, knowing only that he had to stop her, he spun and grabbed the door handle. He twisted it and flung it back, yanking the upper hinge of the door from the frame and leaving the whole thing at a crazy tilt as he dashed through. The icy, predawn air engulfed him. He leaped from the porch to the walkway, the flash of headlights seeming to pin him in midair for an instant.

"Bonnie!"

He grappled for the gate latch, kicking at the crossbar, and pushed through. She had backed the Suburban into the street, turning it sharply so that its headlights shone west. Spikes of golden light were inching over the eastern horizon, streaking the pale gray sky vertically. He ran through the slush of snow and mud to the street.

"Get out!" he demanded, even as the door swung slowly toward him. He grabbed its edge and pulled it back, then stepped around it to reach inside. His hands closed in her sweater, and he got a fleeting impression of a pretty mouth rounding in shock as she twisted to face him, her foot descending toward the ground. He hauled her out and pulled her against him. "You are not leaving me!" he said. "And damn it, lady, you are not divorcing me. Period!"

For an instant she said and did nothing, her eyes locked on his face, mouth ajar. Then suddenly she melted against him, her arms coming up and and about his neck.

"We're not even married yet." She was smiling, and her eyes glittered brightly.

"Well, we're going to be," he grumbled. "But you damn sure better know what you're getting into because you are never—repeat, never—getting out." She laid her head on his shoulder, and he felt the moisture of tears spreading in the fabric of his shirt. "I couldn't stand it," he admitted, holding her tight.

"I'll never leave you," she whispered, "now that I really have you."

"You always did," he told her, "but I just this minute realized it."

She hugged him tight. "Thank God!"

He held her against him, watching the golden sun creep over the edge of the world, and thought, *This is going to be incredibly wonderful.*

"Worth all the gold and silver in the world," she told him, as if reading his thoughts. "I think we should call it The Painted Lady."

"What?"

She drew back and looked up at him. "The lodge. We should call it The Painted Lady. You know, the nickname for these old Victorian houses."

He couldn't believe she was bringing this up now! "That's the most ridiculous thing I've ever heard."

"I beg your pardon?"

"I just agreed to marry you!"

"And I couldn't be more delighted!"

"So suddenly you think you can rename my lodge?"

"*Our* lodge."

"Okay, *our* lodge. That still doesn't give you the right—"

She went up on tiptoe and brought her mouth hard against his, arms flinging up about his neck again. His body responded immediately, tired and emotionally drained as it was. He groaned, knowing he was and would always be defeated by the sheer joy of what he felt for this woman.

"Damn that Harvey Pendergast," he said, tugging at her hair to pull her head back and free his mouth. "I'm going to kill the creep for getting me into this."

"Owen!"

She was frowning, so he grinned. "Right after the wedding. First I need him for a best man."

She laughed and started babbling about all the plans they had to make, but he wasn't listening. He was thinking. Some tough guy he was. All it had taken to upset his safe existence was one bright, breezy, beautiful woman—correction, the *right* bright, breezy, beautiful woman. Now it was a crapshoot again. She could leave him, but she could stay, too, and for this woman, this one woman, it was worth the risk. Because he loved her.

Some tough guy he was.

*   *   *   *   *

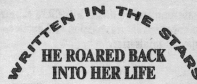

WRITTEN IN THE STARS

HE ROARED BACK INTO HER LIFE

Max Rafferty was the quintessential Leo. Proud, charismatic, and when it came to love, he was a LION ON THE PROWL— August's Written in the Stars selection by Kasey Michaels.

Max couldn't understand why Julia Sutherland had left *him*. But when he discovered their divorce was invalid, Max knew it was time to turn on the Leo charm... and win Julia back!

LION ON THE PROWL by Kasey Michaels... only from Silhouette Romance in August. It's Written in the Stars.

Silhouette Special Edition

presents

SONNY'S GIRLS

by Emilie Richards, Celeste Hamilton and Erica Spindler

They had been Sonny's girls, irresistibly drawn to the charismatic high school football hero. Ten years later, none could forget the night that changed their lives forever.

In July—
ALL THOSE YEARS AGO by Emilie Richards (SSE #684)
Meredith Robbins had left town in shame. Could she ever banish the past and reach for love again?

In August—
DON'T LOOK BACK by Celeste Hamilton (SSE #690)
Cyndi Saint was Sonny's steady. Ten years later, she remembered only his hurtful parting words....

In September—
LONGER THAN... by Erica Spindler (SSE #696)
Bubbly Jennifer Joyce was everybody's friend. But nobody knew the secret longings she felt for bad boy Ryder Hayes....

SSESG-1

SILHOUETTE·INTIMATE·MOMENTS®

IT'S TIME TO MEET
THE MARSHALLS!

In 1986, bestselling author Kristin James wrote A VERY SPECIAL FAVOR for the Silhouette Intimate Moments line. Hero Adam Marshall quickly became a reader favorite, and ever since then, readers have been asking for the stories of his two brothers, Tag and James. At last your prayers have been answered!

In August, look for THE LETTER OF THE LAW (IM #393), James Marshall's story. If you missed youngest brother Tag's story, SALT OF THE EARTH (IM #385), you can order it by following the directions below. And, as our very special favor to you, we'll be reprinting A VERY SPECIAL FAVOR this September. Look for it in special displays wherever you buy books.

Silhouette Books®

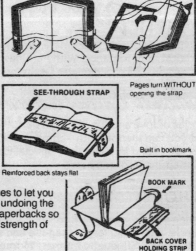

FOUR UNIQUE SERIES
FOR EVERY WOMAN YOU ARE...

Silhouette Romance ®

Tender, delightful, provocative—stories that capture the laughter, the tears, the *joy* of falling in love. Pure romance...straight from the heart!

SILHOUETTE *Desire* ®

Go wild with Desire! Passionate, emotional, sensuous stories of fiery romance. With heroines you'll like and heroes you'll *love*, Silhouette Desire never fails to deliver.

Silhouette Special Edition ®

Stories of love and life, these powerful novels are tales that you can identify with—romances with "something special" added in! Silhouette Special Edition is entertainment for the heart.

SILHOUETTE·INTIMATE·MOMENTS™

Enter a world where passions run hot and excitement is the rule. Dramatic, larger-than-life and always compelling—Silhouette Intimate Moments will never let you down.